A WHIRLWIND OPENER

By K.J. Houtman

Minneapolis, Minnesota

Fish On Kids Books LLC
P.O. Box 3
Crystal Bay, MN 55323-0003

Website address: www.fishonkidsbooks.com

Library of Congress Control Number: 2010932549

ISBN: 978-0-9828760-0-8

FIRST EDITION 2010

Manufactured in the United States of America

It is my heartfelt desire to thank everyone that has offered help and encouragement in the creation of Fish On Kids Books, however, the list is long and thereby a testimony to the numerous blessings in my life. To those left off this list I humbly apologize. To the early readers and encouragers, without their enthusiasm this would have been an experiment only and never reached reality: Dave Wendelschafer, Bill and Julie Stephani, Roger Elias, Mack Hedquist, Andy DiMatteo and Cheryl Brandt. Huge thanks to Kay Wendelschafer for the nugget of the idea. To my writing mentor, Jane Resh Thomas and all the wonderful writers at Writing in the Woods, thank you for your gift of the craft and the willingness to share it with me. If this work falls short of the lofty goal of perfection, and it most certainly does, the failing is mine alone. I thank Kim Nermyr, Chris Clemens, Jeff Whiteside and Scott Milawski at Reflections for their creative contributions and quality production. What a gift to work with such talented and wonderful people. To my family I thank God for each of you and hold you in my prayers daily. Thank you for your encouragement, love and support. And to all the fishermen and hunters whom I have had the privilege to know over my long career in the sportfishing and hunting industries, thank you for sharing your love and passion for the outdoors.

Chapter 1

"Katherine Peterson?" The substitute teacher's voice sounds like fingernails on a chalkboard. How does she do that? Mrs. Harsh, with a lipstick smudge on her teeth and breath that smells like milk a few days past its 'use by' date, hands the envelope to Katie. "Remember, don't open it yet."

"Yes, ma'am."

"Douglas Rivera?" Doogie struts up to the front of the room to get his packet. Nobody calls him Douglas.

"Thank you, Mrs. H." Brown-noser. When their regular teacher is around, Doogie's even worse.

"C. Gustav Roberts?" Oh no. Gus slinks down into his seat, willing it away. It isn't what's in the envelope, nothing wrong with that. Their regular teacher, Mrs. Kaye, has given a writing assignment. The assignment is in the envelope.

"C. GUUU-STAV ROBERTS?" Louder, higher pitched. Several of his classmates turn to look at Gus, now quite aware of how much he misses Mrs. Kaye. He leaps from his seat for fear Mrs. Harsh will say it again, or worse. Just get it over with—the sooner the better.

He returns to his desk with packet in hand, the computer-generated label in bazillion-sized font affixed to the front, turned inside toward his body. Mrs. Harsh finishes handing out the packets with Donald Zimmerman.

"Alright everyone. Do not open your packets until after school is out, that is Mrs. Kaye's special request for you. Each assignment is slightly different with different due dates, so read your instructions carefully."

Oh, that voice. One more minute and Gus' head is going to explode. The bell rings and everyone stands up and darts for the door. Voices clatter and clang as a sea of fifth-grade surliness departs on a Friday afternoon. "Class dismissed." No one can hear her.

Lots of kids hurry around Gus, but he takes an extra moment to stop and think of all he needs from his locker for the weekend. Friday folder. Notebook. Math book. Big white envelope. Lunch bag. Jacket. Backpack. All set. He walks to the bus, confident that he has everything and he won't need a diversion back to the school after he gets home. Estimated time of departure is 4:45 with his grandfather, Pops. They have big plans for the weekend. It's the opening of fishing season in Minnesota tomorrow, kind of a big deal around here.

"Hi, Katie. Did you look at your assignment yet from Mrs. Kaye?" Gus starts a conversation with a girl in his class that rides his bus as they both jump aboard route 101.

"Not yet. You?"

"Nope. Net yet," replies Gus. "The opener's tomorrow, so I'll look at it later. We're heading up to Leech Lake this afternoon so we'll be all ready first thing in the morning."

"Why do you go to Leech Lake, Gus? We live on Lake Minnetonka, just fish the opener here, silly!"

"My dad is guiding four guys from Chicago that book with him every year. Mr. Schafer likes to fish Leech on the opener, so we use our family cabin."

"I guess," replies Katie. "But it seems a little silly to me to go from one lake to another for fishing opener."

"Maybe. I guess I'm just lucky that I have two lakes to fish on."

It's crowded already, but they find two seats together and sit down amongst the noise. In a moment the bus driver pulls ahead and enters the yellow parade out of the circular drive and toward the stoplight. Even first and second graders are ready for a weekend. Lots of fun voices fill the air. Check that. There's one loud voice Gus hears that doesn't mean fun; Matt Driver, his neighbor, and a grade ahead.

Talking with Katie (or anyone, really) is a strategy Gus finds can lead to an incident-free ride home on the bus. It works sometimes. Other times, there's just no stopping him. Kids jump like grasshoppers to a new spot if a sixth grader wants their seat, and that's just what happens today. Matt Driver moves into the seat behind them.

"So, Roberts, your name isn't Gus after all." Matt Driver sneers when he says it. Katie sighs and turns to look out the window. "It's C. Gustav Roberts! How about that for a funny name." He looks around, trying to build comrades.

"Leave it alone, Driver."

He laughs. "Goooo-stav!"

"Maaaatth-eeeeuw, knock it off!"

"And what's the initial C for anyways? Let me guess...Charlie Gustav? No, that's not it. I can see it in your face."

"LaLaLaLa—I can't hear you."

"Cameron, Craig, Christopher?" They reach their bus stop corner and the boys walk to the front of the bus.

"Stick it in your ear, Matt, and I mean it!" Gus is walking ahead of Matt Driver, but turns back so he doesn't say it too loud. No fighting on the bus.

"None of those either, eh?" He says it all friendly-like as the boys hop down the steps. The bus driver doesn't have a clue what's going on. The door closes and Gus and Katie exchange a look through the window, as the bus pulls away to the next stop. "Well, you've got those slanty-eyes, Roberts. Let's see, maybe its Charlie Chan or CungFu or China Boy."

"I'm serious, Driver. Knock it off you dumb-as-a-rock idiot—or else!"

"Stick it in YOUR ear you little piece of CRAP." Driver shoves Gus from the back as an exclamation point. It's a hard shove and Gus falls forward, the palm of his right hand catching most of his weight. He hits the loose gravel, scraping the skin and embedding tiny stones in the now red flesh. "Hey, maybe that's it. Crap Gustav Roberts." He laughs as he walks the other direction toward his house.

Chapter 2

There is a woodpecker making a ton of racket near the dock. He's just a little guy but boy-oh-boy can he rattle on the trees. His breast is white, and his black wings have small white spots, and a little red cap is perched on his head. He's a downy woodpecker and sounds like a machine gun on the tree. Dut-dah-dah-dah-dah, Dut-dah-dah-dah-dah, Dut-dah-dah-dah-dah.

"Hey Pops, we ready to rock and roll?" Gus neatly stacks the last of his gear in his grandfather's float plane, hearing the sound and spotting the little downy nearby.

"Momen-tari-lissimo." Pops walks over to the cargo door of the plane. "Whew-doggie, look at all that stuff," he says with a whistle, admiring how organized an 11-year-old's packing can be of tackle boxes, rods and reels, backpacks, and duffel bags. Pops tosses his bag in and it lands half-way to Sunday on the pile. "My duffel's 15 pounds. What's our cargo weight?"

Gus can't help himself. He stops what he's doing and straightens the bag so it sits neatly on the pile. "Fifty-five pounds, and with your bag that makes seventy pounds, sir." Pops was an officer in the Navy, flying fighter jets off aircraft carriers. He's a tough old bird, especially since his wife died, Annie's mother. All that was about the time Gus was born, and then he moved in with them. Pops is a little bit old fashioned in more ways than one. He has his own way of saying things, too, and the older he gets the more unpredictable that's become.

"We good?"

"We're good," Gus answers, knowing Pops is expecting a cargo weight summary before take-off. He walks the fuel dolly back to the shore. Ka-lunk, ka-lunk as the wheels cross over the boards on the dock. "She's topped off with fuel and we have over 100 pounds to spare." Mom and Dad are already at the cabin since yesterday, with their customers arriving this afternoon from Chicago.

"Check that pulley right there," as Pops points to a spot just under the wing. "That needs complete free movement so the flaps'll move properly. This control here," as he gestures to the black lever in the center of the console inside the plane, "is what drops the flaps."

"Mm-hmm." His eyes don't follow the pointed digit, he's looking into the water.

"HEY!" Pops explodes, zero to 60 in 2.5 seconds. Gus bristles with the stern rebuke of a single syllable and snaps to attention. "This is important stuff ya' need to know about flyin' and is key in a pre-flight routine. You check ev'rythin' once, and most things twice. You got it? It's a heckuva lot more important than fishin'."

"Yes, sir. Sorry." Gus reaches over and tests the pulley. "Moving free and clear."

"Alrighty then. Maybe we'll practice a little bit more today to make sure you know how to handle the controls on this girl, see if you've been payin' attention or not, or if your head's in a fishin' magazine while I'm talkin' to ya." Pops harrumphs and walks around to the left side of the plane to climb in. Gus hops in the right side and buckles up his seat belt.

Pops flips switches while looking in a spiral bound book. Then he takes a break from the pre-flight routine and softens his tone. "What is the matter with you today? I thought you were dab-near jumpin' outta yer skin, itchin' for the season to start. Now you seem all down in the dumps. What's up with you?"

"Aw, it's nothing."

"Nothing? You sure?" Pops looks hard at Gus but his words are soft. A small shadow, maybe just a twitch, crosses Gus's face.

"I am excited about the season opener—I really am. Honest!" Just that fast it's gone. Gus smiles with straight white teeth and big brown eyes that sparkle when he speaks. Whatever was there is gone now.

Gus is excited to get out of town, that part is true. But it's not just the thrill of the new fishing season. After what happened after school today, just as important is getting a break from Matt Driver. He stirs up trouble as easy as a witch stirs up a Halloween brew.

The initial wasn't even a big deal, not nearly as big of a deal as it could have been. Just a little piece was enough to set things in motion. What would it be like if the whole thing got out?

Gus had thought hard and fast about coming up with a swing after Driver's shove. He could land a punch that would give the jerk a bloody lip at least. He wasn't afraid of a fight, even if Driver was bigger. But he pushed down the urge to take it to the next level. Not worth the trouble if there's a real fight, especially on such an important weekend. Definitely not worth getting grounded from the opener.

A few days away will be just the ticket, doing the one thing that Gus loves, fishing. Watching TV shows about it, reading magazines about it, and of course, actually fishing. Gus is already a better fisherman than his brother Jake, who's five years older. That drives Jake crazy but Gus l-o-v-e-s besting his brother. And he's nearly as good as his dad. Not too bad for a fifth grader. One day he dreams to be a Champion and win fishing tournaments, and everyone will ask him how to catch the big one.

The engine revs and the propeller kicks to a start, spewing popping sounds as it starts its rotation. Within a few short minutes the plane taxis away from the dock. Pops lines up the right position for take-off on the water. "We don't need no stinkin' runway, right?" Pops smiles as he says it, hoping to lighten the mood.

"Just a stretch of water. Let's rock and roll!" The two high five as the take-off begins, just as much a part of their ritual as checking pulleys or filling fuel tanks. Water sprays from the chop of the waves clear up to the windows, enough to turn on the windshield wipers.

Chapter 3

Pops has Gus ease the throttle up, it's not the first time he makes him help fly the plane. The engine screams to a pitch that nearly hurts the ears. The plane races across the water—like a big clunky boat, not a sleek speedy boat. Pontoon floats, like magnets on Mom's refrigerator, cling to the water. Faster and faster, until it feels nearly out of control, the wings are sure to break apart.

It jostles left and right, water splashing, wind fighting against the wings. Gus holds his breath when it gets to this part...until... the plane lifts into the air as Lake Minnetonka loses its hold.

In the blink of an eye everything that felt completely wrong turns completely right. This is not a boat for the water. This is a bird for the air, what it's meant to be. Everything is right in the world, and the speed is perfect now. It doesn't feel too fast anymore, and no windshield wipers are needed. Gus' stomach settles down. It's like going to the edge of scary and back, a fun kind of scary.

In just seconds they're skimming over the tops of the oak, maple and willow trees, now fully green in May. Only the catalpa trees are slow to leaf out and might fool one that didn't know they aren't dead, just the last to arrive, like Jake sleeping in on a Saturday morning. They all seem so close you could reach out and touch them.

The blue water below displays ripples of waves that crest in short white tips, like a moustache left behind after a glass of milk. There are hundreds of waves with hundreds of white streaks.

Gus smiles thinking of milk moustaches everywhere and tucks away the trouble he's leaving behind.

Jake can't go this weekend since he has to work. The pangs of growing up and responsibility kick in when you're almost 16 and need money to buy a car. He's old enough to take care of himself alone, but Mom worries he's old enough to get into trouble, too. Jake is staying over at Grandpa Bud and Grandma Dee's house for the weekend. This will be the first opener Jake misses with the family. He probably doesn't care. He thinks more about cars, girls, and wrestling than anything else. He won at State finals in his weight class—as a Sophomore! Everyone's talking about whether he's good enough to wrestle at the University of Minnesota or maybe Iowa. Pops loves wrestling.

"Al and Alma's," Gus spouts off like he's filling a square on a bingo card as he looks at the sites below. No one's standing on the upper deck of the big dinner boat cruiser. It's just too cold and windy. "Big Island. Arcola Bridge." Gus calls out landmarks as they go.

"Lush and green, ain't it buddy-roo," as Pops admires the Lafayette club. Everything is finally green and the golf course is beautiful with the criss-cross cut fairways and various circle-shaped greens. Minnesotans wait a long time and endure harsh winters, when green season finally gets here everyone's happy.

"It's great."

"Right as rain."

"No volleyball games at Lord Fletcher's." Lord Fletcher's is a big restaurant on the lake with lots of boat slips, but just a handful of white cruisers are moored up to the pier today. On warm summer days almost everybody goes there when boating on the lake. "I love their wings and fries the best, and the pink slushy lemonades." Gus is hungry just talking about it.

The guys settle in for the 90 minute flight. Before long, they're out of the Twin Cities and over farm country, with dark black fields waiting for green shoots of corn and beans to sprout up.

Gus grabs his backpack from the floor near his feet and pulls out the envelope that he received at the end of the school day.

He wonders in anticipation about Mrs. Kaye planning secret and unique projects. The only clue he has is that it is a writing assignment. He rips the end of the envelope and Pops looks over at what's going on.

"Whatcha got there?"

"I don't know yet. I mean, all I know is that it's a writing assignment from Mrs. Kaye. But we had to wait until school was out to read the instructions and find out more details." Gus tips the envelope sideways and the object lands on his lap, a leather-covered notebook with an embossed jig on the front, the type you might use for fly-fishing. Gus rubs his fingers over the indentations on the soft brown surface, feeling the rise and fall that outlines the hair-jig that would surely entice a nice trout from a rushing stream. Opening the cover Gus sees light green ink-lined pages, the little jig faintly appearing at the beginning of each page.

It is so cool.

It takes a few moments to leaf through and look at all the empty pages. Maybe there's something written somewhere? He turns page after page. Nope, all empty.

"What is it, a journal?" Pops watches as Gus turns pages.

"Yeah. Isn't it awesome?"

"Looks pretty fancy. What's yer assignment?"

"I don't know. There's nothing written in the journal. Let me check the envelope again." Gus picks up the big white envelope and peers inside. A single white sheet of paper is tucked along the inside. "Here's something."

A computer printed note:

Dear Gus,

As you know I've had a family emergency and called out-of-state for a funeral. I wish I could be there to give you this in person, but sometimes things happen beyond our control, and we need to step up to the plate for the other people around us. You know me, I'm always full of baseball analogies in life.

But you, Gus, are always full of fishing analogies, and when I found this journal I absolutely had to get it for you. I hope you like it.

Your assignment is to journal for 30 days. Not what happens in your life or what you do each day. Perhaps that could be a journal for another time. THIS journal will be you teaching the reader the most important things they need to know about fishing. You always talk so smart and knowledgeable about all the "stuff" around fishing. Tell your imaginary reader all about the terms and the how-to. Perhaps they will learn to enjoy the sport that you love so much—that is, if you show the magic in addition to the information.

Thirty days means it won't be due until the last day of school. So take your full month.Have a great fishing opener (hey, I did good to know that much, right?)

--Mrs. Kathleen Kaye

P.S. I know that people don't always like to talk about IQ or "brain-power", but I have seen what your potential is Gus, and while I would NEVER call anyone lazy, I do want to encourage you to make this work the best that you can produce.

"What does it say?" asks Pops.

Gus is so struck by the note from this wonderful teacher, he's not sure how to respond.

"What's the assignment, buddy-roo?"

"Um, to write about fishing for 30 days, teaching someone that doesn't know anything about it."

"Write about fishin' for a month? Ridiculous. What's happenin' to our schools these days. Sheesh."

Gus closes the journal back up and once again is struck by the simple beauty of the brown leather journal and the intricate design of the fly on the front.

Pops and Gus travel along in an easy silence. It doesn't matter if Pops doesn't understand, Gus does.

Chapter 4

"Look—an eagle!" On the left side of the plane, Pops points.

"Wow, look at him soar. He's beautiful. Hey, that reminds me. I have a question."

"Fire away, buddy-roo," says Pops.

"Why do woodpeckers peck on a tree?" That little downy has been busy outside their house the last few weeks.

"Well, woodpeckers are doin' several things by peckin' on trees," answers Pops. "First, they use their call and the noise on the tree for markin' out their territory and for mating."

Weird. Okay.

"They're also hungry little buggers—lookin' for food," continues Pops. "Woodpeckers eat termites and other insects found on and in trees. Makin' holes allows 'em to find those little critters that live inside the wood. They often holler out a hole to make a nest with their peckin'. The little bits of saw dust fall creatin' a soft, cushy nest bottom." Pops says holler but probably means hollow. He has his own way of talking that takes a little getting used to.

"What's their group name?" It's a game Gus plays called three-in-a-row, quizzing each other on what birds, insects, or animals are called. Sometimes it's group names, sometimes it's male or female names, and sometimes it's the baby or adult names.

Mostly bird groups are flocks. But there are a few exceptions, and some groups have special names.

"A group of woodpeckers is a descent," answers Pops. Wow, Pops is pretty smart. "How about geese?" He launches a round of three-in-a-row at Gus.

"A gaggle," Gus answers, thinking he's glad he works on this stuff.

"Pheasants?"

"A bouquet, if they're flushed." Gus is two out of three so far.

"Right-o. One more, let's see if I can stump ya'. Teal?"

"A spring of teal, YES!" Gus pumps his fist in the air getting them all right, and the last one was a tough one. Pops didn't get him this time, but sometimes he does. He hates getting any wrong, and loves it when he knows stuff that grown-ups think he won't.

"I'll have to work on findin' some harder ones for ya." Gus smiles and looks back at Pops, planning more study this weekend to be ready.

"What do you think of the new spinner rigs that I made up?" Spinners are baits made with one or two hooks for holding a night crawler, called a crawler harness. Gus adds really cool blade and colored bead combinations. Several are wrapped around a foam piece of noodle and packed in the back of the plane. He cuts up the kind of noodles you use in the swimming pool or lake to stay afloat, about 10 inches works great, wrapping the spinners around with the hook piercing the foam to stay neat and organized.

Gus wants to catch a limit of walleyes or maybe catch a nice big trophy fish that all the guys will talk about all weekend—a walleye, northern pike or muskie. Bringing in the biggest fish of opener would be s-w-e-e-t. He daydreams all the time about catching big fish and having all the other guys ask him how he did it.

Maybe one day Pops will brag about the size of a fish that Gus will catch. On second thought, probably not. A compliment from Pops is as rare as a twelve pound walleye.

Just about the time Gus figures the TV network folks will be calling any day for his own show on Saturday mornings, Pops brings him back to reality that he's got a 'heckuva lot more to learn about both life and fishin', before he starts tellin' other people how to live.'

Fishing is the only thing that Gus has found so far that's hard. Really hard. Everything at school is easy, although he wouldn't tell anyone else that. Maybe Mrs. Kaye has figured him out, her note kind of sounds like she has. Who knows, maybe it'll get hard next year in sixth grade. If he tells anyone they might just pile on more work and then he'd have less time for outdoor fun. Ug. Who would want that? Mom and Dad tell him he's doing a great job when he gets his grades and has his parent-teacher conferences, and they leave him alone.

Well, maybe one thing is hard at school, but that's all Matt Driver's fault. Making friends can be a little tricky. It just seems like Driver always stirs up trouble and then Gus just tunes everybody out. Everybody.

"What do you think? Pops?" Gus tries again, but soon realizes that something is very wrong.

Chapter 5

"Are you okay?" Gus is shouting now and even shaking Pops to wake him up. "Hey—WAKE UP, COME ON!"

Gus can hardly think the words, let alone say them. Is he... dead? His stomach flips as he swallows the bile that lurches up from his gut. This just can't be! Looking closer, Pops' chest is still moving, and his eyes flutter. When his right hand tries to lift up from the controls, it appears he's trying to say something. Gus breathes a small sigh of relief, at least he's not dead. "Oh my gosh, Pops, are you okay?" *Dear God, please let Pops be all right.*

Suddenly, perhaps as he's trying to move, Pops' arm and shoulder falls forward and slams into the controls, forcing the plane into a nose dive. Plunging toward the ground, the plane banks to the right all on its own, as the pressure pushes Pops into the door. Gus hears a crack as Pops hits his head on the window, hard. Good thing they have seat belts on or they'd be tossed about and thrown into the roof of the cockpit. Gus' backpack flies up and hits him in the chest.

"O-w-w-w." complains Pops, but it's actually a good sign to Gus. Talking is awake and awake is better than anything else right now, definitely better than you know what. And at least he's not slouched over pushing on the controls any longer. Gus has got to right this plane—NOW!

From somewhere deep within, Gus realizes that this is all up to him. *Okay, so I thought things were a little too easy. I didn't mean I wanted this!*

"Nose up," Gus calls as he pulls on the controls, not sure if one syllable now from his grandfather means he's fully back to reality, but glad for something. "I can fix this. Good thing you taught me all that stuff."

Gus keeps the tension hard on the controls to stop the dive. Pops was right, sometimes he was only half-listening. Think, Gus, think. It's in there somewhere.

"You okay? How about we do this together?" Gus glances over, checking on Pops. It takes all his strength to get the nose up and straighten out the dive. The steering wheel digs into the cut-up palm on his right hand, stinging the tighter and tighter he grips the black plastic. This takes more strength than landing the nine pound northern pike from last summer, times three.

Pops pulls himself away from the door and focuses his eyes on the controls. Deal with Pops or fly the plane? "I could use a little help here. You okay?"

Pops points to the altimeter. "Level, here." He's coming around, but his voice is not the same as usual, more like he has a mouth full of oatmeal.

"Got it, at least I think I got it. Is this okay?" It feels like the plane is level and the indicator's steady at 2000.

"Radio." Pops reaches for something in the center of the console, his hands moving in slow motion.

"Radio, got it." Gus fingers the radio controls and draws on a memory of Pops using it—hundreds of times. Pushing through a moment of tongue-tied panic, Gus gives it his best shot. "Mayday, Mayday. This is One Niner Zulu." 19Z is Pops' call-sign, and that's the way he says it. "Mayday, Mayday. This is One Niner Zulu." Mayday is the universal call for help. Gus says it calmly, but inside he's rattled.

It doesn't take very long until air traffic control calls back. "One Niner Zulu, this is Brainerd Center. What's your mayday, son?"

"Something's happened to my grandpa, and he's sick. I know a little bit about flying the plane. I just leveled out a dive. We dropped quite a ways but I think she's level. Pops needs help, but I gotta fly the plane, too."

Gus tries to keep the panic in check. Does he sound like he's about to throw up? Does he sound only 11 and scared to death, positive there are skid-marks on his tighty whities?

"You got it, buddy, we'll help you down," air traffic control responds. "What's your name and how old are you?"

"My name is Gus and I'm 11 years old." Now they know.

"Okay Gus, my name is Al. Can you tell me your GPS coordinates and your altitude right now?"

"Pops is a little too old fashioned for GPS in his plane, but the altitude is 2000, which looks like 2 o'clock on the dial. Does that sound right?"

"Okay, Gus. You're doing great," answers Al from Brainerd. "What kind of plane are you flying? Do you know?"

"It's a Cessna 172 float plane, a four-seater."

"Okay, a float plane. That changes things. Where'd you come from and where are you heading?"

"We left Lake Minnetonka about 5 o'clock and we're headed to Leech." Gus looks over at Pops. He nods his head, and brings his left hand up to the spot that hit the window. That's a good sign, he's with it.

"Two dials to the left is your air speed indicator. What's that?"

"The air speed is 45 knots." Gus must have been paying attention by more than a half when Pops was teaching him before. Thank goodness.

"Throttle up a little more power. Your air speed is a little slow, and I don't want you to stall. Throttle up, okay?"

"Okay," Gus says through the radio, hoping that he knows just what to do next.

Chapter 6

"Crap. Is this a stall? Pops, is this...? Oh CRAP!" The plane begins to shudder and shimmy.

"Too slow. Stall. Add power." Pops' speech is still slow and halting.

"We've got a problem here, Al," Gus continues on the radio. Crap. Take care of Pops. Talk on the radio. Watch all the controls. Fly the freaking plane. So he wanted life a little harder?

"What's the matter, Gus. Is everything okay?"

Pops points at a control and says, "Power."

"Okay, adding power—CRAP!" Two geese are right in their path and Gus hard banks the plane to avoid hitting them. But he doesn't get the power added, and the plane continues to shudder....too slow to fly and drops like a rock.

Gus looks over at Pops and then out the window and scans the scene below. A lake is right in front of them, a small lake, not Leech, but it will have to do. "I see a lake below us, Pops."

"Yes. Tell them."

Oh yeah, the radio. "One Niner Zulu, we're in a stall and I gotta put it down." Throwing up is definitely an option, too.

"Okay, Gus," replies Al at ATC. "What's your altitude now?"

"1800 feet and dropping fast, a lake is below, I'm heading for it."

"Watch your altimeter and use your yoke to keep the nose up. Just line the plane up so you have plenty of room on the water. You'll be landing at 1400 feet or so. When you approach the lake, just keep it above the trees and then once you pass the trees put the flaps down and it should drop right down the last 50 or so feet. OK? You got it?"

"I think I've got it. I've practiced landings with Pops. I guess this is one of those times that he was planning for."

"I guess it is, Gus. You're doing great."

"My hands are sure sweaty, Al. I think I've gotta put the radio down and concentrate. I'll still be listening, though. OK?"

"You got it."

"On the water," says Pops.

Gus gets very serious about lining up the plane for approach on the small lake.

"I can do this, right?"

Gus looks over at Pops, who nods with his reply. "After trees, flaps down."

"Clear the trees, just clear the trees and drop her down." Gus begins a mantra, talking himself through the process, looking down at the lake below and estimating time to approach the water as they descend. "Am I doing all right?"

"Gus, just remember, keep the trim level and after you clear the trees, put the flaps down. The flaps control is the black handle at the bottom center console." Al's voice at ATC is in the background.

Gus mutters the instructions from Pops and Al as he focuses with all his might. Altimeter. Yoke. Engine power. Flaps. Getting down this last stretch to clear the trees seems to take forever, waiting for the moment when the timing comes together. For now it's watch the dials and wait.

His mind wanders. Up until now landing the nine pound Northern was the biggest thing that ever happened to him. And the biggest trouble in his life was Matt Driver giving him a hard time. Now it's up to Gus to save their lives.

And suddenly, the wait to clear the trees is over and he's just above them. They look so close. Yikes. Does he time this out okay? Is he too high or too low?

"Clear the trees and drop the flaps. Clear the trees and drop the flaps," Gus mutters out loud. He drops the flaps. It feels hard, like a rubber wall and really fast as they approach the water and Gus' heart is in his throat. He can't even breathe or swallow or say a word. All the words are stuck inside his worry. The waves splash up on the windshield, and the wind jostles the plane left and right. Uh-oh! Are they down? Are they in one piece?

The floats of the plane are on the water, and once again the craft feels like a clumsy boat, jostling left and right as the speed and the water fight for control. They're down, but the tree lined shore is just ahead. There are no brakes in a float plane, how the heck does he stop from crashing into those trees?

Just then Pops stomps on a rudder pedal and the plane turns abruptly port-side. That definitely helps to slow it down. If only the lake were a little bigger. As they reach the shore, a tree branch crashes through the windshield, shattering plastic and scattering shards everywhere in the cockpit. A smaller portion of the branch whips Gus in the face, lashing his cheek. The big branch snaps off, just short of whacking Pops straight on.

Close call. They're on the ground and the sound of the engine and prop are loud. He reaches over and pulls the red knob. Soon all is quiet, and the stillness hangs over them, limp and disconnected—like the severed tree branch that dangles in the cock pit, removed from its life-giving trunk.

The only sound is the waves on the shore until the radio breaks the silence of the moment.

"You…it…us." It's Al at the Brainerd ATC, not knowing that Gus is already down. "Clear….and….flap….the…en…..to…line." The radio is breaking up and only transmitting every few syllables.

"I better tell him we did it," Gus tells Pops. "You okay? How bad is your head? What about the thing? The stroke or heart attack or whatever that was in the beginning?"

"T.I.A. Mini-stroke. Had one in March. Will be okay."

"Anything I can do?"

"Radio. Tell your mom."

Chapter 7

"Al, this is One Niner Zulu," as Gus fingers the radio once again, feeling just a little bit older and somehow different from just a few moments ago. "We are down safe and sound." He's not sure how much of his message is getting out. Hopefully Al is getting it all.

"Good…us," in between crackles.

"Thanks, Al. Thanks for your help. Pops says he had a T.I.A. or mini-stroke. I guess he had one in March so it has happened before. He's okay, not great but okay. He hit his head on the window hard. I think he's got a pretty good bump on the head. We took a tree branch through the windshield, but so far, I think that's all the damage. Will you call my mom and dad and tell them we're okay? Their names are Annie and Jim Roberts, and they are at our cabin in Walker. Pops' name is Hessel Riss."

The radio crackles and makes a few "ksh-ing" sounds, but Gus can't even make out Al's voice anymore. Something must have damaged the radio from the tree branch coming through the window. He leaves it on just in case it starts working better.

"I hope it got through." Gus turns to Pops and unbuckles both of their seat belts. "The radio's not working very well. I'll try again later."

Gus hops out on his side of the plane, then comes around to Pop's side and gently opens the door. Pops has just enough strength to pull himself out of the seat, moving carefully around the windshield shards. Gus reaches for a duffel bag and pulls out a t-shirt, using it to sweep the floor at Pops' feet.

"Easy now, just sit down here first." Gus hops up to stand next to Pops, both hunched over as they stand in the shortened height of the cock pit. Gus would like Pops to sit down first on the edge and then dangle his legs out the door, like on the end of the dock, however he's never been very successful in getting Pops to do what he wants before. It usually works the other way around. "I don't want you to fall now. We got this far and I don't need you to break your neck falling out of the doorway."

Pops sits down on the edge. Relief washes over Gus.

"Strength is gone. Tired."

"My legs are a little shaky right now, too. That's okay. We're in no rush. Let's just sit here a second and let me look at your head."

"No." Pops attempts to bat Gus' hand away from his head, but his hand moves slowly. Okay, maybe he won't cooperate. Baby steps.

"I just want to see if you're bleeding or not. I can't do anything to fix a knock to your noggin' anyway—so don't be so stubborn. Just let me see if you're cut. Okay?" He doesn't say anything, but he doesn't flinch or try to stop Gus from looking. "A bump, a good one, and a couple of scrapes, none bleeding anymore. You want to try a step down to the float?"

Pops mumbles something that seems like affirmation. He goes with it.

Gus holds on to Pops' arm as he steps forward onto the float of the plane, holding onto the wing like a railing. He stops to rest, gathering strength for the next step down.

"No hurry, when you're ready." Eventually Pops lets go of the plane and puts one foot down while he leans on Gus. "Steady, take it easy."

Pops walks a few steps away from the plane with Gus at his side, but it takes all his strength and he can't go farther. "Sit down."

"Okay. No problem. Down we go." It isn't exactly graceful, but he's down on a soft patch of grass, leaning against a smooth tree trunk.

Gus exhales long and slow. *Thank you, Lord. Thank you, thank you, thank you.*

"I'm going to go try the radio one more time," says Gus. "I'll just see if Al got my message before that we're okay but we need some help for you, and make sure they call Mom and Dad. You can just rest here for a minute, okay?" It is a rhetorical question and he doesn't wait for the non-answer.

Gus walks back to the plane and climbs in through the side with the least amount of windshield shards everywhere.

"Al, ATC Brainerd, this is One Niner Zulu, over," Gus calls on the radio. He waits for a reply, but instead of Al's encouraging and soothing voice, there are only crackles and static. Not sure if the radio can transmit better than receive, Gus decides it wouldn't hurt for one more try to get their message out. Once again Gus radios that they are safe, to inform their family, and please send help for Pops.

How long will it take for help to arrive? It could be an hour or two or a day or two. Big difference! Gus decides to get busy so Pops can rest comfortably until help comes. They need a cozy spot for the windy, chilly evening, whether help comes tonight or in the morning.

They need a fire.

Chapter 8

"I think a fire sounds good." Gus walks around the area, scoping out a spot.

"Uh-huh."

"But maybe not right here under the trees. We need a place for the smoke to get out." Gus walks around some more. "This is good, and it won't be too far for you to move."

"Okay."

"I've got an idea. Hold on." Gus runs back to the shoreline and grabs two flat stones near the water. "I can use these to dig a hole." Gus is on his knees, bent over like a puppy dog preparing to bury his bone. Luckily, the earth is soft and sandy so close to the lakeshore, so it's not too hard to dig without a real shovel. "I'll scout for firewood," Gus offers when the pit is deep enough. "You okay for a few minutes?"

Pops nods and Gus takes the pushing away gesture with his hands as permission.

Gus looks for twigs, thin and dry, that will light easily, and also dry needles from a few pine trees. Old needles are almost like gasoline on a fire. They're so dry and brittle that they'll make this fire easy to start.

But kindling is only the beginning. He needs some bigger wood to keep a fire going, especially to burn all night. Gus makes a few more trips locating fallen branches that have been down on the ground a long time. He snaps the dry branches into smaller sized pieces by putting one end up on a rock, then jumps with all his weight to break it. Snap. He folds the broken spot back until it snaps apart, and carries the pieces to stack up a nice pile that will feed the fire for the night.

The little lake is tree-lined and firewood is plentiful. There are lots of dead branches and twigs on the ground. Gus sees animal tracks throughout the woods. The dusk of evening is here, and Gus heads back to check on Pops.

"You still doing okay?"

"Yeah, head hurts," speaking slowly.

"I believe you. There's a pretty good bump on your head. And maybe a T.I.A. or mini-stroke doesn't feel too good, either."

"I'll be okay."

"I hope so. Hey, I'm just gathering firewood before it gets dark. You okay here if I keep at it for awhile? I don't want to have to go back out in the night. There are plenty of animal tracks."

"No problem-o." Gus smiles when he hears Pops sound like himself. He is doing better.

"Okay, we'll move you closer when I get done. Just rest for a few minutes." Pops nods his head.

With each trip, Gus organizes two piles near the fire pit, one for kindling and the other for the logs. The pine needles go into the fire pit first and then the small twigs on top. Then throw in a few dried leaves, almost like paper, and spread them between the twigs. Several longer twigs make the shape of an Indian tepee over the top of the kindling. That allows air to get through. Then, when the fire takes off, Gus will add the larger wood and they'll be all set.

"You have matches?" Pops calls out to Gus.

"Pops, do you really think I don't have matches? You saw all that cargo in the back of the plane, right? Remember, I packed 55 pounds of gear, of course I have matches. You never know when you're going to need them for a shore lunch, or if you need to burn the end of a rope to keep it from unraveling."

After Gus locates the tackle box with the matches, he lights the kindling. It is a beautiful sight as it takes off. Right away it makes Gus feel like he's doing something good. The fire will provide light and warmth all night long, and a fire is a good way to keep animals away, too.

Soon the fire licks up the sides of the wood. The kindling is spent and the longer logs are hot on fire. When the teepee of wood crumbles into a pile on the bottom of the pit, Gus adds the larger logs that will burn hot and for a long time. They're set for the night. Good thing, it's getting late.

"Nice fire."

"Let's move you a little closer to the warmth, it'll be dark soon."

"Yes," he answers back, but he needs help as he tries to get up. No problem. Gus doesn't mind if Pops leans on him. "This feels good," and he even smiles as he sits by the fire. Gus is relieved and glad to hear Pops sounding better.

"You doing okay?"

"Better," he says slowly as he reaches up to touch Gus, who meets his hand and sits down next to him. It feels so good to snuggle up next to his grandpa. They sit that way for a l-o-n-g time while the sun sets across the lake. They watch the fire burn orange and bright as the logs crumble a little bit more. Sparks fly as moisture and tree sap snap and pop in the heat. For a little while, though, they can pretend that everything is okay.

Chapter 9

As the fire cools, Gus carefully moves away from Pops to add more logs, glad that the pile of wood is large and nearby with dark setting in.

"You hungry?"

"Thirsty."

"I've got some stuff in my backpack. I'll get it." Gus walks away from the fire, missing its warmth and light with each step. Jumping into the plane he looks in the glove box for the flashlight and finds it. Shining the light over the duffel bags and interior of the cockpit, looking for his backpack, he realizes something useful, and starts ripping the cushions off their seats.

"How about something soft for tonight?" Gus lines up the seat cushions to make a mattress, next to the fire. "Hold on, there's more."

More trips, more stuff for cushy bedding for the night. "Here's a jacket for you." Gus helps Pops put it on, but can tell by Pops' movement that he's better. He can put both his arms through the sleeves.

Between sweatshirts, duffel bags, jackets and seat cushions their campfire has a messy, lived-in look already, like they've been there days not hours. "And finally, ta-da!" Gus pulls out the food treasures in his backpack. "A beef stick, granola bar, and two SOBE Life Waters, Fuji Apple Pear flavor." It's like hitting the lottery.

Pops mostly just drinks one of the waters, but chews on a bite size piece of beef stick when Gus breaks off a hunk and hands it to him. Gus can tell by his voice that he's getting better. His speech is clearer and he sounds more like himself.

"So what's a group of woodpeckers called?" Pops surprises Gus with a round of three-in-a-row. Wow, he must be feeling better. "See if you learned anything today."

"Oh, I learned more than a few things today. Like how to land a stalled airplane after your Pops has a mini-stroke. How about that one?"

"Yes, you did. You did a really good job." Amazing. A twelve-pound walleye when you least expect it.

"Thank you, sir. And it's a descent."

"So you were listening—for once." Definitely getting back to normal.

"How about that."

"Bats?"

"A colony." Bats eat a lot of bugs, especially mosquitoes. Gus hopes there are bats around, it will make for more of a pleasant under-the-stars sleeping experience. Good thing he has bug spray along.

"Fish?"

"That's too easy—a school." Gus laughs.

"I know, I'm tired and my head hurts." His voice is getting better, though.

"That's okay, you can rest now." Gus gets up and adds a soft duffel bag filled with socks and underwear under Pops' head for a pillow.

While Pops sleeps Gus unzips his backpack and retrieves the leather journal. Opening it, he contemplates for a moment what he will write in it. Teach someone about fishing? There's lots of directions that could go. And who is this someone? Teaching Mrs. Kaye or an imaginary reader? Who would be Gus' imaginary reader? Who would Gus like it to be?

Someone his own age, definitely. It would be easier to talk to someone that's a kid like him. Start with the basics for someone that doesn't know a whole lot, but might be interested to learn. Someone like…Katie? Gus thinks for a moment about his friend from school. They ride the bus together and talk quite a bit about things. He knows that she lives on Lake Minnetonka, too, just like him. She could practice fishing at her house, on her dock. And her folks have a boat, so she could get some time on the water away from shore, too.

It's kind of fun to think about Katie as his imaginary reader of his journal, and not so intimidating about what to write and how complicated or how much to tell. After all, there's fly fishing and saltwater fishing and ice fishing. There wouldn't be enough room in the journal for all of that.

What a day! As Gus drifts off, he realizes that there've been a lot of surprises today: Pops getting sick, landing a stalled plane, getting the journal from his teacher, thinking about Katie, sleeping under the stars by an open fire, and a compliment from Pops.

Chapter 10

Startled, Gus wakes up cold. Guess that makes sense since he fell asleep next to a raging fire. He slept so long the fire is next to nothing now. Quickly, Gus pops up and adds some kindling. Once that takes off he adds the larger wood and sits back down to wait for the fire to catch. It doesn't take very long. Soon there is warmth and light that feels good against the cool evening. Still dark, there is a faint hoot of an owl in the distant sounds of the night, and a slight rustling in the trees. Probably just the wind.

Pops is still sleeping, even snoring a little. Good thing Gus is here to take care of him. Once in a while Pops snorts, startling Gus. Maybe that helps keep bears or coyotes away.

Gus lies back down on his t-shirt and sweatshirt lair across from Pops. The warmth of the fire is soothing and he relaxes, looking up through the branches. This world is God's creation. Gus realizes there is a lot to be thankful for: Pops surviving a mini-stroke, recovering the dive and landing a stalled plane, even the branch that shattered the windshield came just inches from Pops' head. Gus feels the scrape from the branch that slapped his face and the one on his right hand from the push from Matt Driver. He and God need a yarp, his dad's word for prayer. He says most folks get prayer backwards. It isn't nearly so much about talking to God. He's not a vending machine that you walk up and put in your two-cents and get what you want. It's more about listening—to His still small voice.

Dear God—Just want to say thank you for the stars in the sky tonight, and the wonderful trees and lakes around us. You're amazing for what you put together, how did you think all this up? Thank you for everything: the good, the bad, and all of it. And now it's just my turn to listen. Amen.

The fire is warm and even the owl and the wind settle into quiet.

Gus wakes up again, only this time something is different, and he can feel it. The fire is lower but not totally cold. He stokes the fire with a little more wood. It is the turn from darkness to dawn. Not sunrise yet, just the shift between the dark of night and light of morning. He looks at Pops, awake.

"Hey," in a whisper.

"Hey back. You doing okay?" Whispers are contagious.

"Better, but I have to pee."

Gus laughs, quietly. "All right, then let's get you up to water the garden."

Pops' turn. "All righty then."

"Yah, sure, you betcha." Gus does his best Fargo imitation as he helps his grandfather up off the ground. His mom teases Pops about his Minnesota accent sometimes, but Gus has never tried that before. Pops is tall and white haired with bright blue eyes, quite different from Gus with brown hair and darker skin. And stupid Matt Driver calls them slanty eyes. What a jerk. There's nothing wrong with his eyes. They're just like his mom's, and hers are beautiful. Annie was adopted as a baby from Korea, she looks nothing like the parents who raised her.

"Hey dare, doontcha know." Pops plays along. Good, he's feeling better and didn't get mad.

They walk quietly to where he can lean against a sturdy tree. Gus walks a little ways away to give him some privacy to do his business…and faces the other direction, just to be polite.

And there he is, with hot steam coming out of his nostrils like the top of a railroad steam engine, so close Gus can see his breathing through the rise and fall of the rhythm in his chest. A young buck, all alone, his spring-time spikes still velvet. Gus is so close that he can see smooth in some places that he's started to rub off. He cocks his head to the side, looking him over, too. He's curious!

He's probably surprised to see eyelashes for the first time up close, and catch a whiff of laundry detergent from his clothing, or the tell-tale beef stick on his breath. What would he say if he could about this? Would he "talk" with his family? I saw a boy today—up close. He smelled really interesting. How would he explain that? How do you explain laundry detergent or a boy's breath to another who's never smelled such things. Or would he just keep it to himself, a little secret from the others.

Brown eye to brown eye in the first-light of the morning they exchange a look and a moment. More steamy breath from his nostrils, it's wet on the tip. *I won't tell if you won't.*

"Okay, buddy-roo." Gus watches the deer's eyes flicker in fright at the sound of Pops' voice. They dart left and right and then he turns, taking off through the trees, small twigs snapping under his weight as he leaves. In a moment even his white tail, perched upright like a quill pen, is no longer in sight.

"Ready to go back to the fire?" Gus helps Pops walk away from the trees and settle back to his seat-cushion spot.

Chapter 11

"Feel better?"

"Yup, thanks."

"No problem. Your speech is better, you don't sound like you have a mouthful of oatmeal anymore."

"Oatmeal!" Pops harrumphs. "I don't know about that! But don't be talkin' bout oatmeal unless you've got some in that backpack of yours. I'm hungry."

Breakfast? Hmm. Well, it is opening of fishing this morning. "You're hungry?"

"I'll be all right."

"What if I went fishing this morning and caught us breakfast? I don't have a pan and oil in my gear, but maybe we could roast the fish over the fire in a rustic kind of way. With skewers maybe?"

"Really? You didn't pack a pan and oil?"

"Pops, come on."

"I think this is one of the first times I've seen you not have somethin' that you wanted. Duct tape or pocket knife or matches. You're a little MacGyver."

"What's a MacGyver?"

"A guy on TV a long time ago that could fix or make things with what he had with him."

"Nevermind on the fishing, I just thought if you were hungry."

"All right."

"All right what?"

"All right I'm hungry, and some breakfast would be good."

"You WANT me to go fishing?" Gus smiles as he says it.

"I'm not gonna beg, Corn Dog," Pops barks harshly.

Instantly the smile is gone and Gus' face turns ten shades of red. "You weren't gonna call me that anymore. We had a deal."

"Maybe I'll call you MacCorn Dog."

Gus bites his lip so he won't say anything, because if he did he would surely spout Mount Vesuvius. He needs a little space from Pops. He's obviously better and getting cranky with this situation. His head probably hurts and he's hungry.

"I'll see if I can catch us some pan fish."

"Good. You got me thinkin' about it already. My mouth's waterin'."

Jumping inside of the plane, Gus uses the flashlight to locate his gear, letting the dark and quiet calm his nerves after Pops' name-calling that hurt so bad. Gus startles a little gopher snooping around their stuff. Mr. Gopher high-tails it out of there, frightened by the monstrous being standing over him.

Gus finds his rod—it's a beauty. These St. Croix rods are quality fishing rods. Guys like Jim Saric and Tommy Skarlis use them in tournaments and on TV shows. Gus got this one from his mom and dad for Christmas and feels like a pro just owning it. He hasn't had a chance to land a big one with it yet. That is the hope for the weekend.

Oh well, he won't need to reel in a lunker for pan fishing. Just looking for some crappies or sunfish will be good enough for breakfast today. Those little guys are fun to catch and good to eat.

With all this tackle, what should he use? He has to stop and think about it for a moment. He finds some Lindy jigs in great colors like orange and pink and yellow. These will work just fine. Ted Takasaki has won a few tournaments on these babies before. They'll work today, too. He looks to the east and sees the orange sky lighting up, and picks an orange jig, to match the first color of the sunrise.

Then he scours in a different tackle box for the secret ingredient, the best pan fish tool ever—Berkley Power Bait

Crappie Nibbles. They come in a small clear bottle with a screw-off top. There are three bottles in pink, yellow, and white. He decides to start with yellow and see what the fish want. Maybe they'll want something else, and he'll have to change.

That's an important thing about fishing. You have to make a plan, and your plan can be based on what you've had success with in the past and on what you know and learn about your current situation. But you have to pay attention to what the fish want, and they will tell you by what they bite, or by what they don't bite. Good fishermen just pay attention.

Gus grabs some weights, bobber stop and slip bobber. Now it's time to get rigged up so he can start finding breakfast.

The orange sky is changing to pink. The wind is down today and the lake is as smooth as glass. There aren't many clouds this morning and it's cool, the fish might want to be in the warm sun today. Gus scans the water, looking for any signs of structure below.

Almost all fish like structure, but especially pan fish like crappies or blue gills. Structure is just something in the water that the fish can hide in and around for safety. It can be rocks, trees, weeds, or changes in the shape of the bottom. Gus sees one or two rocks and logs sticking out of the water. "Knock, knock. Gus is coming for a visit," he whispers to the fish.

Gus puts on his bobber, ties on his jig and adds a weight. He opens up the yellow Crappie Nibbles and puts one on the jig. Whew, get a whiff of that!

Ah, the first cast with his new St. Croix rod. The ripple of the water when his bobber lands sends multiple circular ridges in every direction. The morning pink of the sunrise shimmers on the lake. Everything smells all clean, wet and woodsy.

And though he'd probably never admit it, Gus loves the stink of Crappie Nibbles on his fingers, a smell that is undeniably fishing. Now, if only the fish will cooperate.

Chapter 12

Gus makes a few casts in different directions—some far, some near. Time seems to work in slow motion, pressure that this is fishing for Pops' breakfast when there's nothing else to eat. Nothing! What would Pops say if Gus gets skunked. Never thought you were much of a fisherman, or something like that.

But it doesn't take too long for his presentation to do its job. Fish on. The sight of the bobber underwater is a welcome relief, as it's pulled down and out of sight, so too is Gus' worry. One fish is not skunked. He reels in a very nice black crappie. Breakfast here we come.

Crappie meat is so good that Gus is already excited to eat. He threads the fish through the nylon stringer that he keeps in his tackle box, replaces the Crappie Nibbles and casts back to the spot that he caught the first one. Catch them first, clean them second. All things in their proper order.

Gus reels in his line slowly. Sometimes he stops, and just lets the bobber sit very still, and then gives a little tug to tweek the jig at the bottom, just a swish. That's usually when it happens. Buh-bam. Fish on. Another bite. He keeps at it, replacing his Crappie Nibbles whenever they're gone. Sometimes the fish are good at sneaking the bait off without taking in the hook. If time goes by without a bite, he reels in to inspect his jig. Empty? Reload. His efforts are rewarded, and soon he has six. That's enough for breakfast, three each, or four for Pops if he's really hungry. It would be nice if he has his appetite back.

Gus locates the fillet knife in a different tackle box and sets to work cleaning the fish. Head off, just behind the gill, down through the middle. Flip and do the other side. He washes them off pouring lake water from his empty SOBE bottle. He cuts off long skinny green twigs that will work as skewers, green wood so that (hopefully) the twig will not catch on fire, but just allow the fish to cook. Gus sharpens each end to a point with his Swiss Army knife. That too, is kept in his tackle box. He'd love to keep it in his pocket, but there would be big trouble at school if he ever forgot and brought it with him. Big, big trouble.

"You doing okay?" Gus has probably been at the water, between catching and cleaning for a couple of hours.

"Yeah, I fell back asleep for awhile. Felt good, but my head is throbbin' and my legs are crampin' up."

"You still hungry?"

"Yeah, I guess so. You catch any?"

"Pops, did I catch anything? Come on!" Gus smiles. "What do you think?"

"I suppose you're so all-fired up about fishin' on the opener you figured somethin' out. So what have we got?"

"Crappies. Six of them."

"Crappies? My favorite. What's the plan for cooking them?"

"I sharpened these green twigs and figured we'd roast them like marshmallows over the fire. There are some hot coals along the edge that have a lot of heat, but not flame. Should work, want to give it a try?"

"Yeah, I think I'll stand up for a minute and stretch my legs, though. You can roast mine for me. I don't think I can sit like that." Gus is down on his haunches with the long skewer extended over the coals. They've had a fire going since last night at sunset, so there's lots of heat, and the firewood that he added when Pops had to pee no longer has flames. Perfect.

Pops enjoys the first one done, licking his fingers as he eats it with his hands. "Mighty fine breakfast."

"Good, I'm glad you're happy."

"I'm sorry about earlier."

"Don't call me that, Pops. We talked about it."

"I know, I was just crabby from sleeping on the ground and the knock on my head.

"I'd still like to get you to a hospital and have you checked over."

"Oh, those doctors and such, always make a big deal out of nothin'."

"You had a T.I.A. or whatever you called it—a mini-stroke. That's no nothin'. And there's a pretty good bump on your head from hitting the window."

"I'll be all right. The doc tried to talk me into some pills back in March and I didn't want to take 'em. Maybe I'll have to think about it."

"You've got to take care of yourself, you know. Mom can't do it all."

Pops harrumphs. "Your mother has her hands full with you and Jake. She doesn't need to worry about me."

"Right."

They pass the time with small talk, mostly about baseball, roasting the crappie fillets over the coals and eating the white meat with their fingers. Gus and Pops have both had shore lunches before, where you have a pan and oil and fry up your fresh catch. But this is the first time roasting fresh fish with skewers for breakfast.

After Pops is full with two, Gus eats the rest and has a happy tummy. He walks to the woods and digs a small pit and buries the fish guts, looking around for the curious buck. No sign. Oh well. Sometimes you just get lucky. Special memories, like that one, you keep close. He covers the hole with the loose dirt so that it can turn into fertilizer. Some little pine tree will probably grow up healthy and strong in this lucky spot.

As he walks back to the fire, he hears a sound. It's not one of the nature sounds that he knows. What is it?

Chapter 13

What is that sound?

He rushes over to the edge of the lake and looks up. Yup, that is the sound of a helicopter. They're probably looking for them, but they don't see the plane tucked under the tree branches. How can he signal where they are?

Smoke. Gus grabs some wet leaves from the shoreline by the lake and runs back and tosses the leaves on the fire. Immediately smoke, thick and white, bellows up through the trees. "This should help the rescuers spot us."

"Not bad," answers Pops. "You could also get the flare gun," he points at the plane. Of course there's a flare gun in the plane!

Gus runs back to the plane to locate the emergency kit. The flares are right where they're supposed to be, just the way he likes it. He runs back to Pops to ask about using them.

"Go stand by the shoreline and shoot straight up over the water. Just keep away from the tree branches so it has a clear shot up." Pops shows Gus how to use it. "And don't aim right at the helicopter if you see it, you sure as heck don't wanna hit him with a flare."

Gus walks over as instructed and aims straight up. The chopper has to be somewhere in the vicinity, but he can't see it directly overhead.

"Now?" He shouts from over by the water.

"Dab nabbit, Gus. Shoot the darn thing."

Like firing off a pistol, Gus shoots the flare into the air, hoping the pilot will see their mark and return to their spot.

In just a few moments, the black whirly-bird descends from above over the little lake. Closer and closer to the calm water it descends, making a circle of ripples on the water's surface, the downward wind sending water spraying off the surface. Gus jumps up and down, waives his arms and hollers, "Over here! Over here!"

And then they see him. Two pilots, both wearing headphones and sunglasses, although the windows of the helicopter are dark and it's hard to see inside. It looks like one pilot makes a motion with their hand—like 'thumbs up'.

"I saw them." Gus runs back over to Pops by the fire. "But they left again."

"I suppose to find a place to land."

Gus hadn't thought of that. The helicopter can't land on the lake. It's not like Pops' plane with floats and the shoreline is way too crowded with a lot of trees. Gus starts doing little things to get ready to leave their camp. He picks up the seat cushions, sweatshirts and other clothes that were laid out to sleep on and puts them back in the plane. He puts away his fishing tackle, and spreads the coals around in the fire pit with a stick.

Soon he hears the sound of footsteps on the wooded forest floor as twigs and branches crunch underfoot. "Hessel? Gus?" A girl calls out their names.

"We're over here," Gus shouts loudly. The girl, with a long brown ponytail sticking out of her navy blue cap, arrives with a guy wearing the same style cap. Both sport navy blue flight jumpsuits with patches all over and carry a couple of packs.

"We're glad we found you guys," she says. "Everyone has been worried. Thanks for the flare. How are you doing?" She looks at Pops.

"We're doing okay," says Gus. "Are you a nurse? Can you take a look at Pops? He's the one that had the mini-stroke, and he konked his head, too."

"We sure can," says the girl, smiling and looking at Pops. "Hi Hessel, my name is Justine, and this is Jeffrey. We've been looking for you and I'm glad we found you. I'm not a nurse, but Jeffrey is. He'd like to check you over. Is that okay? And then I'd like to take all of us for a little helicopter ride to the hospital. How does that sound?"

"YOU are the helicopter pilot?" asks Pops. "And HE'S the nurse?"

"Yes," answers Justine, smiling, and we all chuckle—even Jeffrey.

Gus realizes that he was thinking the same thing that Pops said out loud. Think first, talk second is the golden rule. Pops goofed this time, not Gus.

"Come on, Gus," Justine says. "I want to see the plane and hear all about your ride yesterday. Let's give Jeffrey some time alone with Hessel." Gus and Justine walk over to the plane under the tree branches and leave Jeffrey and Pops by the fire.

"So this is why we couldn't see the plane during our search," says Justine. "You skidded right up on shore and nestled under these branches."

"How did you find us?"

"I saw some smoke and needed to check it out," answers Justine. "Either man-made or natural, I'd need to investigate, since I put out forest fires, too."

"You do?" Gus looks at Justine, noticing that she is very pretty. A girl that flies helicopters to rescue people and puts out forest fires, too. Amazing.

"Yes, I do," answers Justine. "I'd need a different kind of helicopter equipped with water to dump for a fire. But either way, I came over a little closer to the smoke. I just didn't see any gleaming sheet metal or a section of a wing, so I thought perhaps I'd widen the circle when you shot off that flare. That was smart."

"Thanks."

"That flare helped me zero in on your location, and when I brought my helicopter down closer—there you were."

"I'm glad for help for Pops. He's doing pretty good, but I'm glad we have a nurse now."

"Jeffrey's a great nurse. Now, tell me about your flight yesterday.

What happened to your grandfather, and how you ended up here? Luckily, I might add—all in one piece!"

"Well," Gus starts. And then he tells Justine all about their departure from Lake Minnetonka, how Pops got sick, and then falling forward into the controls and Gus fixing the nose dive. Then there's the may-day call on the radio, talking to Al at ATC, the stall, the geese, and then putting the plane down safely, except for the branch that shattered the windshield to shreds. It's quite a story and it takes awhile to tell. Justine is very interested in what Gus has to say. He was just getting to the part about fishing for breakfast when Justine interrupts.

"You were very smart, Gus, and brave."

"Aw…I don't know."

"And how old are you, 11, right?"

"Yeah."

"I don't know of too many 11 year olds that could do what you did yesterday. How hard was it to fix the dive?"

"I had to use all my strength to get the nose up."

"I bet you did. And how about the stall and the geese?"

"The plane shimmied and shook in the stall."

"That's called buffeting."

"Huh, buffeting. Okay. Then Pops hit his head. He was conscious but he wasn't exactly able to help much. I think he was seeing stars."

"Or tweeting birds." Justine and Gus smile thinking of a cartoon movie about Roger Rabbit. "So you handled the aircraft, Gus. That's a pretty big deal, and you didn't panic."

"Oh, I was nervous and scared all right. But Pops is always teaching both me and my brother about his plane. He expects us to pay attention and learn. Looks like I was listening along the way."

"Definitely." She gives him a pat on the shoulder for a job well done.

Jeffrey walks over. "You ready to get going? I'd like to get Hessel checked into the hospital for a few tests and make sure he's comfortable."

Darn. Gus was just about to tell her about the Crappie Nibbles secret weapon for pan fish and how he found some nice structure to catch six crappies.

"Roger that," says Justine. "Come on, Gus. Grab what you want to carry with you. Let's get the stretcher set up, Jeffrey."

"What will happen with the plane and all our stuff in it?" Gus is gathering water in his empty SOBE life water bottle, and heading to the fire pit to douse it thoroughly before leaving.

"Don't worry, Gus. This is a pretty remote spot. We had a hard time finding it, and we were looking for it. I think your stuff will be okay for a day or two. We'll figure out something to come back."

Chapter 14

Gus isn't going to leave his St. Croix rod and his favorite tackle behind, even if there are just bears and raccoons around. He's gathering stuff up along with his backpack, and can overhear the conversation between Jeffrey, Justine and Pops.

"But Hessel, it's at least a half-hour walk back to the chopper. That's too much for you."

"I don't need a dab-nob stretcher."

"How old are you, sir?"

"What the heck does that have to do with anything?"

"I'm just asking, sir. Would you ask a man of your age that had a T.I.A and then probably a concussion to walk out under his own power? Through the woods no less? Or would you insist that he ride on a stretcher?" Jeffrey is trying to win the argument. He doesn't know how hard that is to do. Nice try, though.

"Hessel, your grandson, who's 11, just landed YOUR plane. If you were healthy that wouldn't have happened." Justine's entered into the attempt.

"It's embarrassing to be carried."

"Not a soul will know or see. Besides, the FAA is going to be on your tail after this. You want to show that you are being a cooperative good pilot so that you can get your medical rating back."

Justine got him on that one. He won't want to give up flying and will do whatever it takes to get his medical back after this fiasco.

"I'll just close my eyes and think of it like a hammock, you two swaying me in the breeze for nap."

"That works for me. You too, Jeffrey?"

"Saddle up, let's go."

Pops gets on the stretcher and really does close his eyes. He can't look at the people carrying him through the woods or he'd probably jump right up. There's no way an old guy could traipse through the woods after all he's been through. He needs medical attention and Jeffrey's a nurse that knows what he's doing, but it isn't easy talking Pops into anything.

"Want me to take a turn?" Gus asks, thinking he's only schlepping his own gear. Not exactly a three-way split in duties.

"No, that's okay. We train for this," Jeffrey replies. Justine must train for it, too, because she looks fine holding up her end of the stretcher.

As they walk through the woods Gus keeps an eye out for his friend, Curious Buck as he's now named in Gus' mind. No sign, but perhaps he's watching from a safe distance.

When they get to the helicopter it looks HUGE sitting in the middle of a meadow, like a super ginormous dragon fly from the future. Jeffrey and Justine let Pops climb up to the back on his own, knowing they pushed it enough on the stretcher ride. He can manage the last couple of steps.

"I'll need you to rest on the gurney back here," Jeffrey tells Pops as he organizes the bed-on-wheels in the back. "This way they'll be ready to take you into the hospital when we land."

"I'd rather sit up front with Justine." Pops attempts to argue but Justine just gives him a look. "Oh, all right." He lies down on the gurney and Jeffrey gets out some medical supplies and works on Pops.

"What kind of helicopter is this, Justine?" Gus gets to sit in the front left spot. Pilot in command on a helicopter is the front right.

"It's a Bell 429," answers Justine. "One of my favorites to fly. It's strong and fast and can hold a lot of cargo, like all of us!"

Gus puts on his seat belt while Justine begins her pre flight routine. She fusses with levers and switches—inside and out.

"So what's the pre-flight routine on a helicopter, Justine. I've watched Pops with the plane."

"Three main things: make sure the controls have free movement, add battery power so there's electricity for the instruments, introduce fuel to the engine to get it started. Pretty similar to planes."

As Justine is doing her steps, Jeffrey, who's in the back by Pops, hollers "Gus!"

Gus turns toward the back and he hands him a cell phone. "Someone wants to talk to you."

Who could this be? "Hello?"

"Gus, oh thank goodness you're all right." It's Annie, his mother. "I have you on speaker phone, and your dad is right here, too. How is Pops? Are you okay? We've been so worried."

"We're fine, Mom," Gus answers, realizing that they probably experienced a lot of worry over the night. "Did the ATC reach you? Tell you we landed okay?"

"You are awesome," adds Jim. "I'm so proud of you for landing the plane. You're very brave and smart."

"Thank you, Dad," Gus replies, swelling with the compliment. It makes him feel like he can be like him one day, because his dad is brave and smart. "Do you know what?"

"What son?"

"We're in a helicopter right now with a girl named Justine. She's our pilot and she's going to fly Pops to the hospital. How about that!"

"That's great," answers Dad. "Your mom and I are almost to the hospital now, too. We'll see you when you get there. Enjoy your ride."

"All right Dad, I will."

"Ready for take-off," Justine calls. "Can we stow the cell phone and get this bird in the air?"

"Roger that. Dad, I need to go now. Justine's ready to leave and the cell phone needs to be off. I'll see you soon."

"Tell Pops that we love him," says Mom. "Good-bye."

"Bye," Gus says and hands the phone back to Jeffrey, who

stows it in a zippered pocket of a flight bag. "Mom and Dad say 'hi,' Pops." Gus doesn't want to tell him that gushy stuff.

"Phone is off and stowed Justine," Gus tells her through the headset. "We're ready, right, Jeffrey?" Gus looks at Jeffrey and sees his body tense up while he's speaking.

"That's right," says Jeffrey in nearly a whisper. These headphones are really cool. It isn't loud with them on and you can just talk and not shout. Gus realizes he was too loud a minute ago. Now he knows.

"Okay, here we go," says Justine. She clicks the switches and moves levers, and before you know it they're above the ground. She slowly turns the helicopter in a circle—a 360 she calls it. When all is clear, they're flying through the air.

Chapter 15

The helicopter ride is awesome. Gus has been in small planes with Pops his whole life, but being in a helicopter is really different. In a plane you're always speeding above everything. In a helicopter, though, everything seems slower. Gus looks around at the land and lakes below them. He can see a lot more details.

"There's Pops' plane," but he remembers to use a normal voice.

"Wow, Gus, you're eagle eyes," says Justine. "I should take you with me when I have search missions."

"I just knew the shape of the little lake we landed on. I don't think I'll ever forget that."

Gus looks down at the lake, spotting where he caught the crappies just a little while ago. He can see parts of the plane through the tree branches, since he knows what he's looking for. No smoke from the fire, which is good. They doused it before they left.

And along the water's edge is his forest friend, Curious Buck, getting a drink of water, but lifting his head at the sound of the rotor blades above. Still curious.

"Well, Gus," asks Justine through the headset. "What do you think of your first helicopter ride?"

"I love it. But if something happens to you, Justine, like it did with Pops, I don't think I could put this safely on the ground. I don't understand what you're doing to fly this."

"That makes sense, Gus," answers Justine. "Hessel taught you about the yoke and rudder with a plane, so you knew how to control it. He also showed you some of the most important gauges so you'd learn about altitude and air speed. It's not too much different on a helicopter—just a little. Let me show you."

"All right."

"The most important parts of a helicopter are the cyclic, the collective and the pedals. The cyclic is this stick." Justine gestures to the controls between the pilot's legs. "It controls all forward, backward and side-to-side motion."

"So the cyclic is what you use for forward, backward, port or starboard?"

"Right, although aircraft are not like boats. We just say left and right, not port and starboard."

"Oh."

"So you're a boater?"

"Yeah, I love time on the water, especially fishing."

"That's cool. I fish a little bit, enough to know that it's fun when you're catching fish, and boring when you're not."

"True that."

"Then there's the collective. That's located here." Justine shows Gus the control to the left of the pilot, in the center between the two seats. "It controls altitude—up and down motion."

"Okay, cyclic for forward, back, left and right and collective for up and down."

"Right. And then the anti-torque pedals on the floor." Justine has both feet on pedals. "This is a little harder to explain."

"Yeah, because we already have all the directions covered with the cyclic and collective."

"Exactly. The pedals basically control the direction the helicopter is facing."

"Which way it's facing?"

"Yes, because the rotors are turning, right? We can choose which point in the 360 we want the front of the cockpit to face."

"Oh, I get it. You don't have to move the helicopter to have it face a different direction, you adjust with the pedals?"

"Right. You're pretty smart, Gus."

"What is torque, Justine?"

"Torque is the measurement of force the blades have on the helicopter. Because we have torque we need these anti-torque pedals to keep the part we are sitting in to not rotate."

"Cool. Is that the hospital?" Gus points to the right.

"Yup. Do you see the big H on the roof top with the orange wind sock? That's the heli-pad. That's where we're landing."

Gus looks down and sees cars pulling in and out of the parking lot, people walking on the sidewalks, even an ambulance pulling away from the hospital's back door. Mom and Dad stand by the door on the hospital heli-pad, waiving. Within just a couple of minutes Justine sets the helicopter down gently. Gus wants to jump out right away but Justine tells him to wait.

"Hold tight. The hospital staff will be out to get Hessel right away and we need to stay out of the way."

"You got it." She's the boss in this helicopter, the pilot in command.

Chapter 16

Gus takes off his headphones and hangs them up in their place in the helicopter. He turns to Pops. "How are you doing?"

"I'm doin' better, Gus," says Pops. "That was a really nice ride, eh?"

"Oh yes. Justine's a great pilot. And based on how good you look, I think Jeffrey's a good flight nurse, too!"

The hospital flight team opens the door and gets Pops out first. They unfold the legs under the gurney and wheel him into the hospital through the big swinging doors. Mom and Dad have a chance to see him and exchange a few words before they rush him away.

"Okay," says Justine. "We're all-clear for departure from the helicopter. But just one thing, when you exit the aircraft stay clear of the tail rotor and just remember to duck."

Gus is only 11, and probably doesn't have to duck his head, but he'll listen to her. She's in charge. Probably good practice so that you just get used to doing it, no matter how tall you are.

Gus hops out (and ducks his head), Mom meeting him with arms outstretched. Dad enters a second later for a group hug. He didn't realize how much he missed them until now, but he did. Mom starts to cry, then it turns to laughter.

"I'm glad you're okay," she says through her half-laugh, half-cry.

"It turned out okay."

"You got a scrape on your face, and on your hand." A mother's eye takes in 'what's different' in 2.5 seconds.

Gus looks at the scrape on his hand, knowing it had nothing to do with the landing, and he can't even feel the scrape on his face.

"It's nothing, Mom."

"I guess you're right in the grand scheme of life," adds Dad in the conversation. "What a time you've had since yesterday! I'm so proud of you, landing the plane and then taking care of Pops. I couldn't be more proud!"

"Thanks, Dad. You know that Pops has always taught us how his plane works, so I knew a little about taking over the controls. But the stall was definitely something new and scary, and then we nearly hit two geese, and I just had to put it down. I couldn't recover. Maybe Pops could have if he would've been 100%, but he wasn't. I guess it all worked out."

"Al at the Brainerd Airport told us that you talked with him on the radio and were very calm."

"He helped for sure, but I wasn't always calm. Did he call you to tell you we were down and okay? I didn't know if our message got out."

Mom's emotions settle down. "He did say that he lost radio contact with you, but that you were down and safe, so I just kept being thankful for that."

"I figured you guys would manage for a little while roughing it if you had to," added Dad. "We were just worried about Pops and what shape he was in."

"Let's go to the Emergency Room." Annie wants to check on her dad.

"Hold on, I need my stuff." Gus runs back to the helicopter and grabs his backpack, tackle box and St. Croix rod. Justine comes over and puts her hand on his shoulder.

"We have to go. Jeffrey and I just got another call and we have another run to make. Great meeting you, and I know that we'll see each other again real soon."

"Thank you, Justine. Great meeting you, too, and I think you're a wonderful pilot."

"And I think you're a wonderful pilot, too. I gotta go, duty calls."

Justine moves quickly to close the cargo door of the helicopter, and she and Jeffrey get back in the front. Gus watches them put on their headphones and sees Justine start her pre-flight routine again. It all looks a lot more familiar this time than before.

"What a cool job," Gus' dad mentions as they watch them take off from the roof top.

Gus thinks for a moment of how kind and well-trained these people are, that he only met them this morning, yet he feels close. What would the world be like if there weren't people like these two, whose jobs were helping others? Helping people they don't even know.

"Let's go check on Pops." Annie talks to the reception area on the first floor, in the back of the hospital where Gus saw the ambulance leaving a little while ago. "We're looking for Hessel Riss?"

"Room 5, through those doors and toward the end, on the right."

"Thank you." The family follows the prescribed route and taps on the sliding glass door that separates the patient area from the center nurses station. Lots of people are coming and going, almost all in scrubs, some blue, some green and some with purple pants and flowered tops. Gus can't tell the nurses from the doctors, they all look the same.

Mom enters first as his daughter. "Come on in," she calls to Gus and Jim.

"How you doing, Dad?"

"Dab nabbit, I'm fine. I wish everyone would quit fussin' over me. Just a little weak, but I'm better now."

"Let's see what the doctors have to say about that. I'm sure they need to run some tests."

A doctor comes in and introduces herself to Pops first, and then the rest of the family. "Hessel, you're actually doing quite well for all that you've been through. From our preliminary screening I would agree that it looks like another small T.I.A., or mini-stroke. The timing of it happening while you were flying was challenging, normally these mini-strokes start and end within 5 to 20 minutes. They don't last too long. But driving a car or a plane as in your case, even a few moments can be long enough for catastrophe. Luckily, your grandson got you down safely. Was that you?" She looks at Gus.

"Yes, ma'am."

"You did a good thing yesterday, taking care of the plane and your grandfather. I have a son that's eight years old and I can't imagine him being able to do what you just did. And you're only a couple of years older than him."

"11."

"I want to go home." Pops will not be forgotten.

"Soon. Let's run just a few more tests and if it all turns out the way I think it will, you can probably go home later this afternoon or evening, and you won't have to stay overnight."

"I'm not stayin' here tonight." Pops is making his presence known in the emergency room as 'one of those kind' of patients.

"Let's hope we can avoid it," the doctor replies. "Meanwhile, let's move you to a regular room while we run the tests so that you aren't stuck in this hectic and small space in the E.R."

"Sounds good," says Annie. "After you run the tests can we chat further about what he can and can't do, follow-up care and that kind of thing?"

"Absolutely. For now, though, we'll send Hessel to radiology and then he can meet you in his room. I'll have a nurse give you the room he's being assigned to. Any other questions?"

"I'm hungry. Can I eat something?"

"Absolutely, after the tests you can have some lunch."

"Any restrictions?" Mom asks.

"No, whatever he's hungry for is fine."

"Then get me a double cheeseburger and vanilla malt."

"I'll have the nurse come back in with your room information. I'll stop by later and we can talk further." The doctor leaves the exam room.

In a few moments a nurse comes in with a slip of paper, with a room number written on it. "We'll return Hessel to this room after his tests," she informs us. "Why don't you wait there for him."

"We will," replies Annie. "Thank you for your help."

"No problem. Okay Hessel, you're coming with me to radiology. Party time." The nurse does a little disco dance as she helps Pops into a wheel chair.

"These blasted hospital gowns are impossible."

"They are universally humbling, my dear."

Pops chuckles, which is a pleasant surprise, especially in a situation like this.

"We'll wait for you in your room, see you there."

"Bring food."

Chapter 17

The gregarious nurse wheels Pops away, laughing. How does she do that?

"Gus, why don't you take your gear and put it in the truck? It's parked just to the right of the front door." Dad tosses Gus the keys.

"Okay. I like Pops' idea about food. The crappies this morning were good, but we didn't have much last night. A cheeseburger does sound awesome."

"All right. After you stow your gear, cross the street to Culvers and bring back burgers and malts for everybody." Dad opens his wallet and gives Gus two twenties. "That should do it."

"Sweet."

"Gus, do you want a nurse to look at your scrapes? I'm sure they would."

"Mom, it's nothing. Sheesh."

"Okay. Just asking. I don't want you to get an infection or anything."

"I'll put some Neosporin on when we get home later. It'll be fine."

Gus grabs his gear and they all walk the hallway together. At the elevator they part company, Gus to the lobby, and Annie and Jim push the call button. "See you third floor room, room 220."

"Hey wait!" Gus calls back to his Dad, who reaches out to stop the door from closing. "Today is opening of fishing. Don't you have clients at our place that paid to go fishing with you? Shouldn't you be there and not here?"

"Well, yes, but they all heard about what happened and they were worried, too. I made a couple of phone calls last night and found another guide to take them out this morning. We wanted to be along during the search for you. But then you were found so early, we just met you right here."

"Wow, Dad, does that mean that you missed fishing on the opener?" Gus teases him.

"I guess it does! This is the first time that's happened since before I was your age."

"Well, I still went fishing this morning," Gus answers proudly, thinking back on how he caught breakfast for him and Pops. "And crappies on a skewer over the campfire taste pretty good." Gus heads down the hallway as the elevator doors close.

Gus walks to the front lobby of the hospital with his fishing gear to stow in the truck. There are a couple of people there with cameras. One is a TV camera with a Channel 11 news sticker on the side, and the others are nice digital cameras. Gus knows a lot about high-end digital cameras because his Dad is a professional outdoor photographer. Jim shoots photos for magazine covers and does camera work for television shows, a lot of them in fishing and hunting.

"Hey! You! Are you the boy that saved your grandpa's life and crash landed a plane yesterday?" One guy shouts as Gus walks nearby.

"Not crash landed," Gus answers. "Emergency landed. We didn't crash anything." Well, the windshield didn't escape the tree branch, but….

Uh-oh. Now they know he is the one, and they're over taking pictures, putting the microphone in his face and asking questions.

Gus isn't sure how much he should say. On one hand, everyone's okay and there might be no harm answering their questions. On the other hand, Pops might get really mad if he's talking about him or his health, and it gets on the local news.

Then one of them asks a question Gus can answer. "Hey kid, why do you have your fishing pole with you?"

"It's not a fishing pole. It's a St. Croix rod," he answers. "I have it with because I went fishing this morning and caught some crappies for our breakfast. It is fishing opener, you know, and it would take more than an emergency landing to stop me from fishing on the opener. I love to fish!"

Everyone laughs and takes pictures of Gus with his St. Croix rod. One guy asks him a little more about fishing and writes down his answers. He leaves the hospital, puts the gear in the truck, and walks across the street to Culver's. Gus can't wait. He didn't realize he was so hungry.

He orders burgers and malts and carries everything back to the hospital. This time he picks a side entrance to avoid the main door in case the photographers are still there. He takes the stairs up to Pops' floor and locates room 220. Soon Pops comes back from his tests and is happy for the food.

"All right, Gus, how about a game of names. We'll do a round of three-in-a-row." Dad helps pass the time while they're hanging out in the hospital room.

"Okay, bring it on, Dad."

"But not groups this time, the female name."

Gus hopes he doesn't ask about dogs. He knows the answer but isn't sure how Mom would feel about him saying it. It's just a name, but he's not ready to test those waters. "Alrighty then, as Pops would say."

"Yah sure you betcha," Annie jumps into the fun, teasing Pops a little bit.

"Female fox?" Dad starts it off.

"Vixen," Gus answers.

"Female deer?"

"Oh, Dad," Gus moans. "That's too easy—doe!" They laugh.

"Okay, I'll try harder. I just figured you were tired. Heck, I'm tired." He laughs and takes a moment to think. "How about a wallaby?"

A wallaby. A wallaby? Silence.

"Well?" teases Mom. "Come on, Gus." She starts singing the Jeopardy theme song. "Duh-dut, duh-dut, duh-dut-duh. Duh-dut-duh-dut-DUT! Da-da-da-da-da. Times up."

"Wait," Gus is stalling now. Thinking. He doesn't know what a wallaby is—and he knows most of the animals in North America. So it's probably from some far away country. Something makes him think Australia or New Zealand. Wallabies go with kangaroos or something like that. That's it. "Jill," he answers.

"Man," explodes Dad. Pops is resting in his bed, half listening, half sleeping. "You got that in the nick of time! Did you know it or did you guess?" He tries to keep his voice down.

"I guessed." He admits it. "I don't really even know what a wallaby is, but I guessed close to a kangaroo or something. And a male kangaroo is a jack and a female is a jill."

"Wow, Gus," Mom says proudly. "I don't know how you do that."

Soon the doctor comes back and checks in with the family. "Well, Hessel, you seem pretty motivated to get home and sleep in your own bed tonight, so we'll let you do that."

"That's good."

"But you need to get in to see your regular doctor at the V.A. hospital in the Twin Cities this next week. You should probably be on a prescription plan to reduce the risk of stroke. Since we're only seeing you here as an emergency patient, I don't want to prescribe it. I'd rather have you work with your regular doctor."

"I can do that."

"Don't just say it—mean it," the doctor replies. She's got his number already. Perhaps he's not the first tough naval aviator that she's had as a patient. "Rest this weekend, nothing too strenuous. I don't recommend any flying until you get a complete and thorough FAA physical."

The whole family cringes with the news. Pops is not happy with anyone telling him what he can't do. He probably shouldn't have been flying after the first T.I.A., but he didn't tell anyone what happened before. This time he can't keep it a secret.

The doctor continues. "I'll sign all the paperwork and a nurse should be in soon to complete your discharge. It takes awhile, so just hang tight." Annie asks a few more questions and soon the doctor leaves the room.

It takes a couple more hours for all the paperwork to get done. Eventually, after haggling over the hospital regulation, they transport Pops in a wheelchair to the door and help him into the front seat of the truck. Mom and Gus sit in the back seat as they drive to their cabin on Leech Lake.

There's a welcome party to greet everyone when they arrive. Dad's client, Wendell Schafer, started off as a customer years ago but is really now a friend of the family. He comes all the way from Chicago to fish with Jim every year on the opener. Sometimes he brings customers or employees, and other times he brings family or friends, or a mix. Mr. Schafer and his friends come to the door upon hearing the family's arrival.

Hugs and hand-shakes abound, but Pops doesn't want any help walking in.

Chapter 18

"I've got it, I'm fine."

"Sure you don't want to lean on my arm, Pops?" Jim tries to help him out of the truck and into the house.

"Dab nabbit, stop all this fussin'. I can walk to the house for cryin' out loud."

"You okay, Pops?" It's Jake, Gus' older brother. He comes over and gives Pops a hug.

"Hey, Jakey. What are you doin' here?" Pops brightens up seeing him.

"I was pretty worried about you two after your wild plane ride yesterday, so the boss gave me off for the rest of the weekend. I rode up with Grandpa and Grandma.

"Hi, Hessel. Hello, Gus. Oh, I'm so glad you're both all right," says Grandma Dee. She and Grandpa Bud are Jim's parents. Pops is Annie's Dad. They're all together along with four fishing customers. It's a full house.

"Hey Buttons, even you came along for a visit." Gus loves little Buttons, she's a Miniature-Pinscher and Grandpa Bud's special little dog. He spoils her to pieces.

Since it's a cool weekend they built a big roaring fire in the great room after their day on the water. Luckily, the cabin holds quite a few guests in addition to their family. Up to eight guests fit so there's definitely room for four with all the extra family around. The living room, dining room, and kitchen open into one great big room with lots of soft furniture and a huge stone fireplace. Mr. Schafer opens the fireplace door and adds another log to the fire. The smell of the hard wood burning fills the air, but there's something else that smells good, too.

"Grandma, have you been cooking and baking today? It smells amazing in here," Gus wants to know. He loves Grandma Dee's cooking; who wouldn't? She makes home-made everything, always from scratch.

"Well, I threw a few things together today while you guys were at the hospital all day. You hungry?"

"Am I hungry? Yes! How about you, Pops?"

"Abso-posi-tutely!"

"How about you take a few moments to lie down in your room before dinner, Pops?" Annie walks over to her dad to help him to his room. "That will give Gus a chance to take a shower and get cleaned up before we eat."

"What? I need a shower?"

Grandma holds her nose. Mom points to the bathroom. Even Jake is laughing. "Seriously, dude, you stink."

"I worked hard for this stink, landing a stalled plane, taking care of Pops, building a fire, sleeping under the stars, even catching our breakfast this morning!" Gus is having fun with the teasing. He's pretty sure a shower will feel awesome. "All right. All right. I'm going."

Annie, Pops and Gus all leave the room. She opens the linen closet door and tosses Gus a big fluffy towel. "Go ahead and take a nice long, hot shower, Gus. I won't get mad like I sometimes do that you're in there too long."

"Promise? Pinky promise?" He makes his mom link her right hand pinky with his right hand pinky, sealing it tight. Mom adds a hug to the deal.

Pops lies down on the bed for a little rest. He didn't realize how good a nice comfortable mattress with blankets and pillows would feel. He's asleep in a heartbeat.

Gus turns on the radio nice and loud and climbs into a steamy hot shower. Shampoo and soap feel great on his grungy body, wafting cucumber and aloe lather. He takes at least a half an hour knowing he won't have anyone pounding on the door to hurry him out of the bathroom. The hot water stings on his scraped face and right hand. No one knows that he got the scrape on his hand from the fight with Matt Driver. They just all think they're both from the emergency landing.

Clean clothes are in his room and he throws the wet towel and his dirty laundry in the hamper. Even clean white socks smell and feel wonderful. A quick dab of Neosporin on his face and the palm of his hand, and he rejoins the crew in the living room. They all start talking at once.

"There's the star," one of Mr. Schafer's friends starts it off.

"Gus, you looked so cute on TV," Grandma Dee adds.

"You've always wanted to be on TV about fishing, Gus. Today you got your wish," his dad joins in.

"What are you guys talking about?" Gus is confused. TV? Star?

"You were on TV just a little while ago, the six o'clock news," his mom tells him.

"Holding your fishing tackle and saying something about, 'it's not a fishing pole it's a St. Croix rod.'" Mr. Schafer smiles when he says it.

"And, 'it would take more than an emergency landing to stop me from fishing on the opener,' or something like that," says one of the fishing guests. "I loved it!"

Gus looks a little embarrassed, but a little excited about the idea of being on TV, just hoping that he didn't look or sound stupid. "Cool, and they got my St. Croix rod and everything?"

"Yup, everything."

"Wow." Gus thinks for a moment that his dream of being on TV and teaching others about fishing just came a little closer. Steps, one at a time. Cool. "It smells like Grandma's been in the kitchen and I'm hungry. Can we eat dinner now?"

"Let me see if Pops is ready." Annie leaves the great room and walks down the hallway. A quick knock on the door and she enters, without waiting for a reply.

"Hey," Pops says.

"Hey, yourself. Feeling up to eating?"

"I was hungry before you made me take a rest, Annie. Let's eat by gum."

"Want help?"

"I can walk down a hallway by myself, and cut my own food and chew it myself."

"Okay, okay." Annie sighs, sounding tired and turns to walk back and join the others.

Grandma has set the table for 11. "Time to eat," she announces, and everyone finds a chair and settles in. There's bear meat roast from Dad's hunt last fall, pheasant wild-rice soup, and fresh walleye fillets along with plenty of potatoes, asparagus, and fresh fruit, and Grandma Dee's home-made buns.

Dad doesn't ask anyone else to take a turn, they all hold hands around the big table and he prays,

Creator God—Thank you for the safe return of Pops and Gus. We're so grateful. We thank you for all the people that helped them along the way and for their own courage and stamina. And now we thank you for this food, Lord, and ask for your blessing. May it nourish and strengthen us. Amen.

Everyone tacks on an "Amen" at the end and starts passing food around and laughing and telling stories.

"I can see by the walleye fillets on the table that you had a good opening day today, guys." Gus has a lot of questions about the opener, but 'didja catch anything' isn't one of them. The proof is on the plate.

There's plenty of chatter amongst the group about fishing, what it feels like when a plane stalls, helicopter rides and hospital tests.

After dinner, the guests and Pops are asked to clear out, but the rest of the family members all chip in to help with kitchen duty. When everybody works together, it's not too bad of a job. There's plenty of conversation while scraping plates, loading the dishwasher, putting away food, and wiping down counters and tables.

"Turn on the TV to channel 11, Jim," asks Pops. "I want to see what they have on the news at ten o'clock."

Shortly the news comes on and the headline story about a plane crash catches everyone's attention.

"What's this about a plane crash?" Pops is alert and watching the news. The more he listens, the more he realizes they're talking about him. Pops harrumphs.

"But we didn't crash," Gus shouts, with a twinge of whine. He and Pops exchange a look. "Just an emergency landing, that's all."

"It's the TV-way of telling a story," answers Mr. Schafer. "They always try to make everything sound dramatic and sensational. 'Plane crash' sounds more exciting than 'emergency landing.' They do it all the time."

They watch and listen, and soon there's Gus on the TV with his backpack, tackle box, and St. Croix rod! "Hey, look, here it is again," one of Mr. Schafer's friends calls out.

Gus can't believe that he's on TV. He looks tall and confident with his rod and reel and tackle box. Maybe even a little bit rough and tough with the scrape on his face. When he hears… 'I love fishing' he turns to his mom and smiles.

"True that."

Everyone claps and cheers after the news moves on to another story. Then the phone rings, and then rings again, and pretty much doesn't stop for the next hour.

Chapter 19

Gus sleeps great that night, realizing how wonderful it is to have a comfy bed with sheets, blankets, and pillows. The next morning is crisp and bright. When he gets up, the guys have already gone fishing. Mom and Grandma are in the kitchen. Pops is sitting by a small fire in the fireplace, and Jake isn't up yet.

"Hello sleepy-head," Mom says teasingly.

"Good morning," Gus replies a little groggily, realizing that he slept too late to go fishing with the guys. Now that's tired.

Grandma Dee hands him a glass of juice. "How'd you sleep?"

"I slept great, thanks." Gus turns to Pops. "How are you doing?"

"I'm peachy keen and happy to be alive buddy-roo." Guess a home-cooked meal and sleep on a comfy bed is just what he needed, too.

The Sunday newspaper is spread out across the dining room table where the guys had breakfast before heading out. The sports section is toward the top of the pile, and as Gus glances over it, something catches his eye.

It's his picture—in the Sunday paper, a big color photo of Gus and his St. Croix rod! He walks over to the table to look closer.

"What's this?" They all laugh.

"Isn't it cute, Gus?" Annie walks over and rests her hand on his shoulder while he's reading. "One of the photographers in the hospital yesterday wrote an article and you made the Sunday paper from the Twin Cities! There's a whole story about what happened. It's actually a rather nice story, and you do look quite adorable."

"Oh," Gus moans. "I'm going to hear about this at school."

"No, it'll be fine Gus," replies Mom. "It should be really fun for you. And you sound like such a professional fisherman."

"Gus is right," says Jake as he saunters into the room, the last one up for the day.

"Oh, I'm sure you boys don't know what you're talking about," insists Mom. "Anyway, how about some breakfast?" Jake and Gus sit down at the breakfast bar that overlooks the kitchen.

Mom heats up the waffle iron, stirs up some batter and cuts up fresh strawberries. Grandma Dee heats up a couple of strips of bacon left over from the breakfast earlier in the microwave. Soon the two boys laugh as they look at each other stuffing their mouths with waffles smothered in strawberries and Cool-Whip.

"Whoops! I just remembered something." Gus runs back to his room and locates his backpack. When he returns he has something behind his back. "Happy Mother's Day." He pulls out the small item wrapped in white tissue paper with a red string around it. It isn't wrapped very well.

"Oh yeah, Happy Mother's Day," adds Jake, a little sourly.

"This is a little something from me and Jake." He offers her the package. She smiles and takes it.

"Thank you," as she gives the boys a hug. "I wonder what it is?"

"You'll find out in just a second if you go a little faster."

"Oh," she coos as she pulls away the tissue paper. "It's adorable."

"The lady told me, I mean, us, that it's the bluebird of happiness," Gus tells her. "Right, Jake?" It's a small glass figurine made of clear blue glass in the shape of a bird.

"Right," Jake doesn't know what to say.

"This is definitely a bluebird of happiness Mother's Day."

"Is it a little different than what you thought it would be?"

"Uh-huh," she says, lost in thought. "I think next year will be a little different again, too."

After they help to clean up the kitchen the front doorbell rings. It's Justine, and she has a different guy with her this time.

Chapter 20

"Hi Justine," Gus runs over to her quickly. "How'd you find where we live?"

"It wasn't too hard, Gus. Your dad is listed in the tourist information as a fishing guide and lodge."

"Oh yeah," he mumbles, embarrassed that he didn't think of that. "Is this another nurse?" He changes the subject.

"No, this is my friend and co-worker, Fred," answers Justine. "And he's also a helicopter pilot and an A & P. Pops knows that means trained in Air Maintenance. Fred, this is Gus."

Fred looks at Gus like he's a dweeb for thinking he's a nurse. The last time she had a guy with her he was a nurse. He feels like an idiot. He forgot the golden rule: think first, talk second.

"We came to talk to Hessel," Justine adds while she walks over by the fireplace. "You're looking well today, Hessel. This is my friend, Fred Hoffman."

"Pleased to meet you, Sir," says Fred as they shake hands. He said 'Sir'. He sounds military, and Pops likes him already.

"Good to meet you, too," answers Pops. "Can you fly a whirly-bird half as good as this girl can?"

Fred smiles. "No sir, she's a much better pilot than I am."

"Now we know you're honest and humble," answers Pops. "I like that."

"We came to see if you want help getting your plane," answers Justine. "I could fly us back to where we were yesterday. Fred can replace the windshield, then I'll fly your float plane out and Fred can bring the helicopter back. We'll meet back here if that works."

"Abso-posi-tutely," says Pops. "Good diarrhea, little lady. Darn good diarrhea." Oh no. Sometimes Pops says "good diarrhea" for "good idea." Gus wants to crawl in a hole and die.

"Okay." Justine and Fred exchange a look, not sure what to make of that outburst. They're not quite used to Pops yet. "We have a car out front."

"You want me to come?" asks Pops. "But I don't rightly think Annie will let me go. Boys, you wanna tag along?"

"I don't think that would be a good idea." Uh-oh. Gus is sure she hates him, and he definitely should not have called her friend, the military helicopter pilot dude, a nurse. Not that there's anything wrong with a guy being a nurse. Jeffrey was a great nurse yesterday. "The lake that you put the plane down on is small," continues Justine. "One of the reasons you skidded up under the tree branches was that you still had some speed and ran out of lake. I probably won't want any more weight in the plane than I have to, so that I get airborne as quickly as possible."

"Good thinkin' Justine," says Pops. "I can see you're a smart girl. Okee-dokey, then how about the boys go along, and they help carry the gear back to Fred's helicopter so we get rid of all the stuff Gus packed in the back. That'll lighten the load, and you'll be up lickety-split."

"Justine, this is my brother, Jake."

"Nice to meet you, Jake. Well, okay, the boys can go, but I'm pretty sure you need to stay here and rest." Annie agrees with that.

At the airport, Justine starts her pre-flight routine on the Bell 206 Jet Ranger. It's smaller than the last one which was designed for medical rescue and transport.

Fred and Justine are in the front seats, and Jake and Gus are in the back seats. This helicopter is not as fast and powerful as the one they rode in yesterday. With four people in this one, it definitely doesn't have the kind of power that pushes you back in your seat—but it's still fun, and is Jake's first helicopter ride.

It only takes a few minutes to get there. Gus didn't realize how close they were to Leech Lake when they went down. The lake they landed on is part of the Chippewa National Forest and there are thousands of acres of nothing but wilderness.

Soon they're on the ground and walking back to the camp site, no easy task with an eight foot windshield. But ropes make it a little easier to carry such a bulky package as they walk. They find the clearing where Gus made the campfire. It looks so different today. Gus spends a few moments covering up the fire pit and erasing their foot print while Justine and Fred take out the old windshield and install the new. It takes awhile. Gus and Jake unload the gear from the back of the plane.

They caulk the windshield into place, and tie ropes on the sides of the plane, pushing it out from under the tree branches. It takes all four of them to push it back into the water, so it's good the boys came along. They turn it around so it's facing the other direction on the lake. Fred pulls it back close to shore so Justine can climb aboard while walking on top the floats. Then he unties the ropes. At the end of Justine's pre-flight routine the prop turns over and it starts right up.

The noise of the propeller is especially loud, tucked into the little space on this lake with the trees close in around the shoreline. She pushes the throttle and crosses the water. As she's picking up speed, Gus holds his breath until she clears the trees on the other side of the lake. It doesn't seem like there's much extra room. Whew. She clears it all. It's a good thing that they took all that stuff out of the plane, and it's now around their feet, and the boys have to schlep it back to the helicopter.

Fred doesn't say much as they walk through the woods, each loaded down with all of Gus' junk. Luckily, between the three of them, they'll make it with one trip. Fred had thought ahead, and brought a big duffel bag that he straps across his shoulders, his big strong shoulders.

The boys fly back to the airport, with no fun instructional conversation about the cyclic, collective or the anti-torque pedals on the Bell. Fred drives the car to the cabin and all three help carry the cargo inside. Pops' float plane is tied up next to the dock.

"Good job, guys," says Justine. "Looks like we've had a productive morning. The plane and all your gear are back. Fred and I had better get going." She looks at Fred with his hand on the door knob.

"Justine, thanks for gettin' my plane back," says Pops. Justine walks over and gives Pops a hug.

"You're welcome, Hessel," says Justine. "I enjoyed meeting you and your wonderful family. I'm so glad that everything turned out okay."

"Thank you both," says Annie to Fred and Justine. "How kind of you to come back and help us."

"No problem-o," replies Justine, sounding like Pops, and they all laugh. "I didn't want Hessel to worry about his plane sitting out there or stress over figuring out how to get it. And of course, I wanted to come say good-bye to our hero and celebrity." Justine walks toward Gus. "You did a great job putting that plane down safely. I'm so proud of you." She gives Gus a hug.

Tongue-tied for a moment, Gus looks Jake square in the eye and enjoys every moment of this hug from Justine, pretty sure that Jake will not get one. She is very pretty afterall and she and Gus are friends.

"Thank you. Let me know if you ever want to go fishing, Justine," as Gus re-finds his voice. "I can teach you some cool stuff and take you to my favorite honey holes on the lake. You just let me know."

"Okay, I'll give you a call." She smiles as she says it.

After that, there are hand shakes and good-byes all around as Justine and Fred leave the cabin.

Gus decides that he's wasted enough of the day without a fishing rod in his hand. He promptly gets organized to get his stuff down to the lake and get some fishing time in.

You can't catch anything if your line isn't wet, no matter what color your lure is.

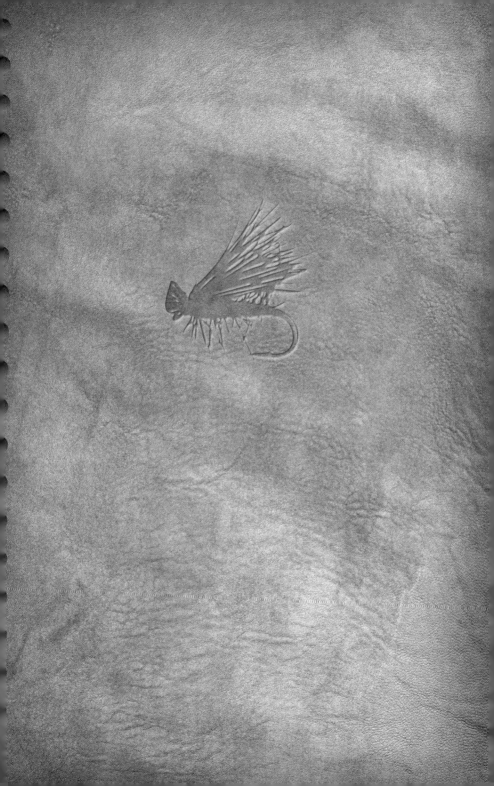

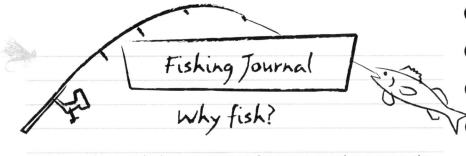

Fishing Journal

Why fish?

Fishing is the best sport EVER because it can become anything you want it to be. Do you want it to be easy? It can be. Do you want it to be hard? Boy, there are times it is. Like when you HAVE to catch just the right kind of fish RIGHT NOW. Like when your grandpa asks for crappies for breakfast, and you only have an hour to get it done. Or if you are in a tournament and you have to catch the best five walleyes you can in just a few hours. That's hard.

Maybe you want to do something that you share with someone else, like a best friend or someone in your family. Fishing can be something special you do together. On the other hand, sometimes you might want to get away from everybody and everything. Fishing can be quiet time alone, too.

Fishing is a year-round sport, so whether you want to fish all year or just for a few months, you can pick. Some people think you have to have an expensive boat to go fishing. Not true. You can fish from shore, you just get more options and more water when you have a boat, but not everybody has one. Don't let it stop you, though, if you don't have a boat.

You might like hockey, wrestling or baseball...me too, but those sports don't provide food for your family. How about that! I love a fish fry!

The most fun part of fishing is the moment that you realize you have a fish on. The tug on your hook, even if you do not actually catch that one and it gets away, is the BEST moment in the world.

Top 10 Things to Get Started Fishing

You will need some basic equipment to get started with fishing. You might not have to buy everything. Ask around and see what you can find. If not, save up your money or ask for some birthday presents or something like that.

1. Rod and Reel. A spincast rig has a push-button for releasing the line. It is the best to get started with when you are new to fishing. Look for a plastic key chain, the type businesses give away (usually for free with their name and address on them) and just tie that on as a plastic plug and practice casting in the yard. Do not buy a rod taller than you are, try to get one the same height as you are. If you cannot get a rod and reel, use an empty soda pop can and wrap your fishing line around the can, just tie the line to the tab.

Spincast Reel

2. Fishing line. Usually new combo reels come with line, but fishing line is an important tool and it is a good idea to keep a spare spool in your tackle box. Start with a monofilament in four or six pound test.

Fishing Line

3. Hooks, Jigs and Lures. Get a variety of hooks and jigs, in different sizes and colors. Ask a person that works at a tackle store and they will get you started with some basic sizes. A jig is just a hook that has a weight built into the hook, and sometimes is painted a fun color or might even have hair attached to make it look more real (like on the cover of this journal). If you have some extra money get some spoons, spinners or crank bait

Jig

Spinners

Crank Bait

lures. The length of the lip that sticks out
the front of a crank bait determines the
depth that it dives. The bigger the lip the
deeper it goes. So use a short lip for
shallow water or longer lips to go deeper.

Spinner Bait

Spoon

4. Sinkers. Extra weights are important so you
can get your bait down where you want it.
Buy a container that has pinch-on weights
in different sizes and you will be ready to get started.

5. Floats or Bobbers. There are two types of floats or bobbers, the
type you clip on and the type your line runs through. Both are
great, and if you have enough money, buy both. If you use a slip
bobber, you will need a bobber stop kit. Slip bobbers
allow you to cast into deeper water further away.
If you are not going to cast far or if the water is
shallow, it will probably be easier to use a clip-on bobber.

Slip Bobber

6. Bait. Both artificial and live bait work great. For live bait start
with nightcrawlers, wax worms, minnows or leeches. If you buy
leeches or minnows you have to remember to take good care of
them to keep them alive. Change out the water and keep them
fresh and cool, otherwise they will just die. Even nightcrawlers and
wax worms should be stored in the refrigerator. For artificial bait
check out the Berkley Power Baits. There are LOTS to choose from,
but here is a tip, I love Crappie Nibbles.

7. Tackle Box. You will probably need a tackle box to keep all your
stuff organized. In addition to the bobbers, sinkers, hooks and
bait in it, you will probably want to put in scissors or a clipper to
cut line, needle-nose pliers to get out a stuck hook, small towel or

rag (hey, it can get messy), nylon
stringer, and an extra cord.

8. Bucket. A bucket with a cover can
   be a seat while you are fishing as well as a place to keep the fish
   after you catch them. However, you don't have to use a bucket. A
   stringer would work for keeping your fish and you could just tie it
   off to a dock or pier, but pack some extra cord into your tackle box
   so you can reach the water with your stringer.

9. Fishing License. Most kids under the age of 16 don't need a fishing
   license, but check with your state as different states have different
   rules about what age you need one. A good place to check online is
   takemefishing.org. They have links to all the states and
   their regulations.

10. Use a buddy system whenever you are by the water, especially
    when you are new to fishing. Ask permission before you go out, so
    the grown-ups know where you are. Only adults should clean fish
    until you are old enough and someone shows you what to do and
    you have permission for filleting the fish.
    Most important is to... **HAVE FUN!**

My Favorite Fishing Knots

Standard Clinch Knot

Improved Clinch Knot

Fish On Kids Books™

Gus' adventures continue with book #2 in the
Fish On Kids Books Series, *Driving Me Crazy*
and book #3 *Spare the Rod*.
Buy them all!

If your club, team, troop or group is non-profit,
sign up to sell Fish On Kids Books to raise
needed cash for your program.

Fish On Kids Books
P.O. Box 3
Crystal Bay MN 55323-0003

Email: info@fishonkidsbooks.com
Web: www.fishonkidsbooks.com
Phone/Fax: (952) 472-1775